THE VENOMOUS MISS VERNON

Miss Blanche Vernon was everything that Ursula was not. While Ursula had been shut away in the quiet countryside, Blanche had been shining in society. While Ursula had been far removed from the game of love, Blanche had been sharpening her skills at winning at it. While Ursula remained faithful to the precepts of virtue and candor, Blanche would do and say whatever was needed to get what she wanted.

Thus the battle for the same man between the dark-haired Ursula and the blonde and beautiful Blanche seemed hardly fair . . . unless Ursula found a way to turn the tables on a rival as ravishing as she was ruthless . . .

NORMA LEE CLARK was born in Joplin, Missouri, but considers herself a New Yorker, having lived in Manhattan longer than in her native state. In addition to writing Regencies, she is also the private secretary to Woody Allen.

SIGNET REGENCY ROMANCE
COMING IN AUGUST 1992

Anne Barbour
A Talent for Trouble

Patricia Rice
Artful Deceptions

Sandra Heath
A Country Cotillion

Georgette Heyer
Lady of Quality

Cupid's Calendar

by
Norma Lee Clark

A SIGNET BOOK

SIGNET
Published by the Penguin Group
Penguin Books USA Inc., 375 Hudson Street,
New York, New York, 10014, U.S.A.
Penguin Books Ltd, 27 Wrights Lane, London W8 5TZ, England
Penguin Books Australia Ltd, Ringwood, Victoria, Australia
Penguin Books Canada Ltd, 10 Alcorn Avenue, Toronto, Ontario, Canada M4V 3B2
Penguin Books (N.Z.) Ltd, 182-190 Wairau Road,
Auckland 10, New Zealand

Penguin Books Ltd, Registered Offices:
Harmondsworth, Middlesex, England

First published by Signet, an imprint of New American Library,
a division of Penguin Books USA Inc.

First Printing, July, 1992

10 9 8 7 6 5 4 3 2 1

For Hilary Ross
My ever-supportive editor

1

My dearest India,

It is with sadness that I write to tell you that my mother passed away a week ago today. There have been so many things to attend to that I have not had a moment until today to write to you. I am so worn down by these past five years attending her, for you know she refused to have anyone by her but myself, and her suffering, poor soul, was so dreadful that it cannot but be a release for both of us. You will, of course, remember that her nature was always somewhat irascible, and terrible pain did not increase her amiability, so that I—

Lady Ursula Liddiard was here interrupted by the entrance of her brother, Rupert Liddiard, earl of Herronly. He was a fleshy-faced gentleman of five-and-thirty years, whose paunch preceded him as he strutted across the room on his unusually thin legs and took up his stance before the fireplace. He raised his quizzing glass and surveyed her.

"Ah, writing a letter, I see," he said, never being one averse to stating the obvious.

"Yes, Rupert," Ursula said patiently. "Did you want something?"

"Dear me, I would not disturb you for the world. Do you go right ahead. I shall be happy to wait."

Ursula sighed, laid aside her pen, and rose. "Nonsense.

You know you will only stand there fidgeting and chuffing until you have my attention. What is it?''

"Well, it is about Albinia. I had a letter this morning and she is very pressing that you return with me. Indeed, she insists upon it.''

"Nothing could prevail upon me to do so, Rupert. You will express my regrets to Albinia and my thanks for the invitation, but as I have explained to you, I must get right away from all my family for a time. I have been tethered here for five long years, seeing no one but Mama and you when you have the time to come—''

"Now, see here, Ursula, if you mean to imply I was backward in my duty to—''

"I meant nothing of the kind, I only—''

"Allow me to finish, if you please, Ursula. As you know very well, Mama quite often refused to see me when I did come. She was never natural in her feelings for her children, she—''

"Please do not say such things now. It is over and she certainly suffered enough pain to atone—''

"I had not finished,'' Lord Herronly said sternly. "The fact is that she was always the most razor-tongued female I have ever met. I cannot remember a kind word from her in my life, and now she is gone, I will not be so hypocritical as to prate on about my grief and so forth. I know she had her troubles with our father, but she had none from her children to deserve her treatment of us. Fact is, she did not have one drop of maternal feeling in her breast that I could ever see. Perhaps with you, as she approached death . . . ?''

"No,'' his sister admitted, for her mother never relented, even when she knew the end was upon her, even knowing, as she did full well, that her youngest daughter was carrying a burden almost too much for her to bear in her constant attendance on the sickroom. Old Lady Liddiard would not allow her two oldest daughters even to come for a visit, nor would she allow any nurses or servants into her room. Only Ursula, she said, did not fret her into fits, though she did not exhibit any warmth toward her daughter for it.

She had despised her son so much, that when he had inherited his title and estates some eleven years before, upon the death of his father, she had refused to remain at Herronly Hall, but had removed herself and her youngest daughter to a house in a town some twenty miles away. There she had alienated all her neighbors and lost several dozen servants before taking to her bed with the dread disease that was devouring her.

"No," continued Ursula, "she remained true to her nature to the very end, poor unhappy creature that she was."

"I am sure you are to be commended for being able to pity her after the years of torment she has subjected you to. However, we've both said enough on the subject. The problem is now you."

"You may rest easy on that score, Rupert, though I am sure I am grateful for your solicitude. However, I do not mean to be a problem, least of all to you."

"Well, of course you are not. I did not mean a problem, but my duty, which I am more than happy to assume. Naturally, you will make your home with me now. Albinia joins me in this."

"But I do not want to make my home with you—at least not just at this present, Rupert," his sister replied decidedly.

"Nonsense. Of course you must. I am in effect your guardian now. Where else would you go? Neither of your sisters is in a position to offer you a home, and there would be a great deal of talk if I allowed you to stay on here alone, unmarried and with no female relative to chaperone you."

"I have no intention of staying here. Why, what would I want with such a house in a town where I know not one single person beyond the doctor?"

"There you are, then!"

"That does not mean, however, that I want to live with you. And since I am of age, I have no need of a guardian and can do just as I choose about my life from now on."

"Then what the devil do you think you will do? If you had taken Batesly when he offered for you, we would not be in this fix."

"Batesly," she repeated in a voice of loathing. "Why, he was senile, Rupert. Not a day less than seventy!"

"Well, you are not exactly just out of the schoolroom yourself, you know."

"Yes, I know that at five-and-twenty I must seem safely on the shelf to you, but I am not quite ready to give up all hope. As for what I will do, I will first make a long stay with my bosom bow, who has been begging me anytime these past six years to come to her. After that . . . well, we shall see. I have Mama's money and a small inheritance from my godmama, bless her, so I need not feel I am cast quite penniless upon the world."

"Who is this friend, may I ask?"

"Certainly you may. She is Lady Swanson, India Allerdyce as was when we were in school together, and she lives in Sussex."

"Why, that must be quite forty miles from here! How will you get there?"

"Please try not to be so silly, Rupert. I shall hire a chaise and take my abigail."

"You surely cannot be proposing to make such a journey with no gentleman to escort you?"

"You may escort me if you insist upon it, Rupert," she replied, her eyes glinting mischievously.

"*I!* Well, I mean to say . . . I could not possibly spare the time . . . all Mama's business to wind up . . . this house and the furnishings to dispose of. And there is Albinia. You know she cannot bear me to be away—she suffers so from her nerves, poor girl—then there is Tom, poor little fellow

. . . fell out of a tree and broke his collarbone, and fretting everyone to pieces: that is why Albinia—I mean . . . not that she would expect you to . . . that is . . ." He floundered to a halt as he met his sister's sardonically raised eyebrow.

After a small silence Ursula said softly but firmly, "You may convey my thanks to Albinia for her . . . pressing invitation, but tell her that I do not mean to make nursing my permanent way of life. I am sorry for poor Tom, and sorry for Albinia's nerves, but I cannot accept the role of spinster aunt at your family's beck and call just yet."

Rupert sputtered and chuffed, but Ursula was not moved from her decision, and though he claimed guardianship, he knew full well that he was in no such position to her and had no way to force her to obey him. To do him justice, he did feel very strongly that as head of the family he must assume responsibility for her, but the devil was in it, in the face of her refusal, to think of a way to make her allow him to do so.

"When do you think to go to Lady Swanson?"

"I should have her reply within a few days, and since I am in no doubt at all about her response, I shall begin packing and be ready to leave as soon as possible after that. It all depends upon my being able to finish my letter to her in time to catch today's post."

Accepting this gentle hint that she would appreciate his absence more than his company, he bowed and withdrew to continue his inventory of his mother's estate.

"Oh, Rupert," she called as he was opening the door, "I hope you will not mind franking my letter for me."

He sighed as one much put upon, but agreed before closing the door behind him.

She crossed again to her escritoire, seated herself, and picked up her pen. As she bent forward to continue her letter, a shaft of sunlight fell across her paper, turning her sleek brown hair to a silvery color. She was a petite young woman, with a trim figure, a softly rounded face, a small straight nose, and a prettily curved mouth. Her best feature, however, was her eyes. They were the deep, clear blue of a summer Mediterranean sky. For all these attributes, she was not a pocket Venus, nor even considered a "toast," but a comely, amiable young woman with a lively sense of humor. It bewildered her family and friends that she was still unmarried, since no one had considered that she would have any trouble finding a suitable husband. Indeed, she had had opportunities, having received four proposals in the two years she had been in society, all of which she had unequivocally declined.

Her mother had not allowed her to make her come-out until she was eighteen; then, when she was twenty, her mother had become too ill to rise from her bed and Ursula had, perforce, to nurse her. The only offer she had had since then had come, through the offices of her brother, from the abhorred Batesly.

Now she rapidly wrote out the substance of her letter and ended:

> . . . so I throw myself on your mercy, dearest India, and pray that you will forgive the precipitateness of my proposed descent upon you. Also I hope you will not feel any need to think of ways to entertain me. Indeed, apart from its being inappropriate for me to go out in company at this time (though I hope you will not be shocked that I am not in deep mourning, for I loathe it and find it very depressing to the spirits), I feel sure that I will find nothing more entertaining than being able to nap away the afternoon upon the sofa with my handkerchief over my face.
>
> I know, my good friend, that I can depend upon you to tell me honestly if my plans do not march with your own, for in that case I can take myself to Brighton or Ramsgate to recuperate and come to you when it is more convenient. I

shall await your response before making any plans, so do not put off writing (for I well know your dislike of writing letters!).

With my best to all your dear family, from ever your loving friend,

Ursula

2

Lady Swanson, upon receipt of this letter, was in transports of delight. She had not seen her friend for over five years. They had kept up their correspondence, two letters from Ursula to one from India, for India was not much of a hand at writing letters, and Ursula was one of the few people to whom she would write.

They had been friends from the age of ten, having arrived, two homesick, frightened little girls, to attend Miss Havendale's Academy for Young Ladies in Bath, upon the same day. Since they were for the most part ignored by the girls already in residence and were wary of their instructors, they had turned to each other for comfort. They were mismatched in size, presenting a picture of contrasts, for Ursula was short and still chubby with baby fat, while India was tall and slender and coltish. The meeting of their minds, however, was perfect and they were protective and supportive of one another, presenting a united front against all the hateful little snubbings and teasings young people can so cruelly inflict upon one another.

They had left the school at seventeen, India to be presented at court and make her come-out at once, Ursula held back at home for a year beause her mother had felt that since she herself had been presented at eighteen, that was the proper age for it. Ursula, who had longed to do just as India did and to share their first Season, subsequently found that it was not too bad to have her best friend a seasoned veteran

of society, who found partners for her at balls and told her
who was who and how to go on.

There could be no doubt that India was a "toast." She
was the sensation of her two Seasons in London, deluged
with partners, posies, and proposals—no fewer than eleven!
After her second Season she had made a brilliant marriage.
It was not the "alliance" her mother had hoped for with a
hovering heir to a dukedom, but no fault could be found with
India's choice, for Robert Youngreaves, earl of Swanson,
was of the best blood to be found in England, young, dash-
ingly handsome, and extremely wealthy.

India sat at the breakfast table now, her face lit with happiness, with Ursula's letter in her hand.

"Robert, dearest, you will never guess!" she cried.

"No, my dear, I doubt I will," he said vaguely, engrossed
in his own post. Then he looked up and smiled as he always
did when he looked at her, for she was so lovely. The sun
streaming into the breakfast-room windows turned the mass
of auburn ringlets that covered her head into flame. Her hair
was so curly and abundant that no matter how tightly she
smoothed it back, nor how rigidly she confined it, within
an hour the tendrils had broken free from their restraint to
spring back into their natural tight curls about her face.

She was a tall, willowy young woman, graceful in all her
movements, whom the new high-waisted fashion suited
extremely well. She had the magnolia-white complexion that
goes with auburn hair, an oval, high-cheekboned face, and
sparkling hazel eyes.

"It is the most wonderful thing . . . well, of course I don't
mean it is wonderful for one's mother to die, though she was
a very difficult woman to get on with and treated all her
children abominably, so one can only wonder if it was retri-
bution that she suffered so much pain . . . though I suppose
I should not say such a thing—"

"My love, I am quite lost in all these circumlocutions.
Please start again. What is the wonderful thing?"

"Oh, did not I say? Ursula is coming to visit at last. Her mother died just over a week ago and she is so pulled down, poor little thing, for, you know, she has had the sole nursing of her mother for five years. The dowager was dreadful to everyone who came near her, throwing things at the servants and using horridly abusive language. Ursula always wrote that her mother could not abide anyone but herself near her, but I would guess there was no one who would put up with such treatment, so dear Ursula had to do it. Oh, I shall take such good care of her—she says she only wants to take naps, and who can wonder after all she has been through . . . oh, and that she will not be all draped in black weeds, for she finds it too depressing—"

"How shocking." This statement came from the side of the table where the dowager Countess Swanson sat, finishing her usual substantial breakfast of a slice of sirloin and baked eggs.

"Why, Mother, I do not think so at all. Ursula has already given up five years of her life to her mother. I cannot see why she should be forced to give up another year for mourning," India said spiritedly.

"I agree," Robert said. "I hate to see young women in mourning, and besides, it is not our business if she does not choose to do so."

"Nevertheless, it is most improper. In my opinion she should not push herself upon you at all at such a time, but remain within the bosom of her family. Why, how are people to treat her when you entertain? It is an uncomfortable position in which to place your guests."

"I am sure they will treat her beautifully. I should not want guests who did not. And she is the most amiable, good-natured creature on earth. Come, Mother, you must not be thinking she is pushing herself upon us, when I have begged her in every letter anytime these past six years to come to me. You will like her enormously, I assure you. Everyone does so. I must go and answer her immediately and have a groom post it at once. Do not leave the house before you frank it for me, darling," she said, planting a kiss upon her husband's brow before dancing from the room.

"I fear no good can come of this, my son," the dowager said portentously.

"Nonsense, Mama," Robert said, turning back to his post.

"Ah, yes, naturally you say so, but you will see that I am right. Apart from everything else, though they may have been friends as children, they must inevitably have gone in different ways since then, leading very different lives, and their ideas will no longer match. She will pull India down dreadfully, which is of all things to be avoided now she is . . . is in an interesting condition," the dowager said with a discreet little cough.

"I doubt anything could pull down India's spirits, Mama."

"You must allow me to know better in these matters than you possibly can, my son."

Robert gathered up his letters and pushed back his chair. "Well, you will excuse me now, Mama, if I leave you alone, but I must see Preevy as soon as may be about Cowl's farm." Robert rarely entered into an argument with his mother, knowing from long experience that it was better simply to make a reason to go away.

The dowager finished her coffee in stately dignity and went away to harass Cook into changing the dinner menu already approved by her daughter-in-law. Since she did this every day, she and Cook were old enemies. Cook listened in silence, nodded as though in agreement, then prepared exactly the menu decided upon by her mistress, the young countess.

The only servants left at Swan Court since the dowager's reign there were the butler, Crigly, and Robert's own nanny. However, they, and all the servants, gave unswerving loyalty to the master and his wife, and listened in stony silence to all the dowager's countermanding orders. If she persisted, they said politely that they would refer the matter to the countess. While frustrating, this never seemed to deter the dowager. Nothing had deterred her from her course in all her life, with the exception of her son.

At his announcement of his impending marriage to India Allerdyce, the countess had been much gratified, for the *ton* had unanimously approved of Miss Allerdyce, who was of impeccable lineage, prettily behaved, and had a nice dowry to bestow upon the lucky aspirer of her hand. She was every mother's dream of the proper daughter-in-law.

However, very soon after his announcement, he had mentioned casually that he thought she should pay a visit to the Dower House.

"I am sure it will need some furbishing up. It has been sitting empty since Aunt Hester died, and she never did much with it while she lived there. Just do whatever you like and send the bills to Preevy."

"The Dower House!" she exclaimed in tones of disbelief. "Are you saying you expect me . . . to . . ." Words failed her.

"Well, of course, Mama. All the dowagers have used the Dower House anytime these last two hundred years. Not my grandmother, since she died before Papa even met you. Where else would you go?"

"But I would not go anywhere. My place is here in Swan Court, as it has been since the day your dear father brought me here as a bride. Who, if not I, should train your wife in the management of this establishment so that she can take over when I am gone? Why, poor little thing, she will not have any idea of how she should comport herself as chatelaine of Swan Court."

Robert laughed. "Oh, you may rest easy on that score. She has been thoroughly trained by her mother, who told me so herself."

"Naturally, she would do so," his mother replied tartly.

Robert laughed again. "Yes, of course she would. Neverthelesss, it is the best way, as I am sure you will agree when you think on it a bit. Two mistresses never work out in one house. And the Dower House is not a mile away, just a step, so you and India can be forever visiting back and forth.''

"Visiting!" commented the countess bitterly. "I never thought I should be reduced to visiting at Swan Court."

Variations on this conversation were repeated every day or so for the next few weeks. Or, more properly, monologues, for though the countess began on the subject, her son seldom responded, only laughing good-naturedly and telling her she would enjoy it once she became used to the idea, and would surely find it very diverting to redecorate the Dower House to her own taste.

She remained unappeased, and just before the wedding she packed and left with a flounce, saying she would seek refuge with her sister in Bath since he would not agree to her remaining in her own house. She went up to London for the wedding, where she tried, unsuccessfully, to cast a damper on the proceedings, and then returned to her sister's house.

This arrangement was very short-lived, for she and her sister were very like in their natures, and her sister was not about to allow the dowager countess to have any say in the management of the house in Bath. Within a month the dowager had taken a house of her own and had remained there until she had received word of India's coming confinement. She had then arrived, bag and baggage, unannounced, upon the doorstep at Swan Court to take charge. That had been two months ago, but she had never since said any word that could lead Robert and India to hope that she would return to Bath. Robert had begun to think about the Dower House again.

3

Ursula's departure for Swan Court was attended by all the discomfiture possible, owing to her brother, who issued contradictory orders to the servants bestowing her luggage on the roof of the carriage, sent her abigail into a fit of the sullens by lecturing her endlessly on her responsibilities for her lady's welfare and jewel case, and reiterating his demands of the coachman to drive slowly until that gentleman irately demanded to be told if he were thought unfit to drive.

All the while, indeed, even after the wheels had begun to turn, pleading with Ursula to change her mind.

"Indeed, indeed, I think you are being too hasty, my dear, and will regret it. After all, to go into company so soon after your bereavement—"

"Rupert, if you want the word with no bark on it, I am not bereaved. I am freed!"

"Hush, my dear, *pas devant les domestiques.*"

"I am sure they all feel the same," she said with a grin.

"Nevertheless, it is not seemly. People will be bound to speak ill of you. Your place at such a time is within the bosom of your family."

Bored by the conversation she had heard far too many times in the past days, Ursula said, "Give my love to Albinia, Rupert. I will write in a few days." She nodded to the footman who held the horses' heads. He let go, sprang up beside the coachman, and they started down the drive, Rupert still protesting. Ursula leaned out to wave, then sat back with a great sigh of relief to at last be out of reach of his voice. She was well aware of the sincerity of his urgings, but also well aware of his reluctance to face the many scoldings he would receive from his wife for having let Ursula escape when she was free at last to be of some use.

Once they were through the town and into the country beyond it, Ursula sat up and gazed raptly out of the window. It had been a very long time since she had seen these vistas, and the ever-changing scenery was delightful to her.

She also enjoyed the bustle of the inn yard when they stopped at midday to change the horses. The innkeeper's wife came out and escorted her into the parlor, where she was given coffee and freshly baked cakes. There was a tiny gray kitten asleep on a cushion of the window seat, and Ursula lost her heart to it immediately. The innkeeper's wife pressed her to take it as a gift, and Ursula was sorely tempted. But good manners prevailed, for to arrive as a guest in someone's house accompanied by a kitten demanding care and attention would be unforgivable.

When they were on the road again, her heart yearned back to the adorable kitten, but after a time she became interested in the scenery again and forgot it. She became sleepy after a few miles, and leaning her head back against the squabs, dozed off, woke when she was jolted, then dozed again. At last an aching neck caused her to sit up and look about. The sun was just above the trees and she was sure they would be stopping for the night soon. Rupert had been so insistent that they be off the roads before sundown for fear of highwaymen, that she had agreed, in order to keep him quiet. He had also chosen the inn, and she had to admit he had chosen well when she was shown into a clean and well-appointed bedroom not an hour later. Carey, her abigail, at once began opening bags, laying out brushes on the dressing table and an evening gown on the bed.

"No, no, Carey, I won't change tonight. I don't think it at all necessary."

"You can't mean to go down to dinner in that traveling costume," Carey exclaimed, much shocked.

Ursula was wearing a dark blue pelisse over a lighter blue silk gown, made up high in the neck and long-sleeved. "I shall simply remove my pelisse, and if you'll take out my Kashmir shawl, that will do very well for dinner in a country inn," Ursula replied firmly, removing her bonnet. "Could you fetch up some warm water, please, Carey, so I can wash away some of this dust?"

Carey sniffed, but did as she was told. When, a half-hour later, Ursula descended to dinner, no one could have faulted her appearance. The gown looked fresh, the shawl was draped elegantly over her elbows, her face glowed, pink-cheeked from a vigorous scrubbing, and her hair shone from its recent brushing.

Mrs. Tottle, the landlord's wife, awaited her at the front of the staircase to escort her into the private parlor. She had smoothed her hair and put on a clean apron for the occasion. "For she's a real lady, she is, Tottle. Her maid says she's a Lady Ursula something, daughter to an earl."

"And a tidy armful, too," responded Tottle with a wink.

"For shame, Tottle, speaking of gentry like that," she scolded, bending to baste the chicken turning on the spit.

He smacked her bottom in a friendly way. "I'll just fetch up a bottle of that stuff I've been saving. Fancy she'll not say no to a glass of that there to her dinner."

"There, now, my lady, don't you look a treat," Mrs. Tottle exclaimed as Ursula descended the staircase. "Might be going to some grand dinner, you might, dressed so fine and all. Just you step this way into the parlor. We've no other guests tonight, so you'll have it all to yourself. Sit yourself down here before the fire and you'll have your dinner in a trice."

Ursula smiled and thanked her and admired the bright fire and the table laid nearby with candles glowing. She sat down before the fire and relaxed comfortably, suddenly feeling tired from her long day of traveling.

There was the sound without of carriages pulling up to change horses, hearty male voices, horses neighing, but they barely impinged upon her consciousness as she gazed into the flames. When the door opened with a bang, she nearly started from her chair.

In the doorway stood a gentleman of medium height, slim and elegant in a driving coat with at least ten capes. He stopped short as she gasped, and removed his tall brimmed hat, staring straight into her eyes with surprise at finding her there. Their gazes locked for a long moment before she dropped her eyes, the color flooding into her cheeks.

"I beg your pardon, madam. I was not aware the room was occupied," he said, making her a bow. She was too confused to think of any pertinent response. "I hope you will forgive me for startling you so." He waited a moment, hoping she would raise her eyes again so that he could confirm their astonishing color.

She murmured something, so softly that he could only make out " . . . please do not heed it . . ." Since she seemed disinclined to further conversation, he was left with nothing to do but retire. He bowed again and closed the door gently behind him.

Indeed, Ursula could not have spoken, though she despised herself for her want of conduct. To blush and mumble so missishly at five-and-twenty was surely ridiculous, but his sudden appearance had startled her so, and then for it to be *him* of all people in the world! For she had recognized him at once. He had occupied her thoughts a great deal during her first Season. He was just the sort of man a young, green girl would be attracted to: slimly graceful, a thin aesthetic face, stormy dark gray eyes. He, however, had had no time for such a dim creature as Lady Ursula Liddiard, being at the time at the feet of Marianne Chaist, a tall, willowy blond who also possessed a staggering inheritance. Not that he had need of her money, being wealthy enough himself not to have to hang out for a rich wife. He did not win her, however, for Ursula remembered reading in the papers of Marianne's wedding to a marquess.

She wondered for a moment if he had married someone else, but dismissed that idea, for she would have been sure to read of it if he had. She had subscribed to all the London papers to read to her mother, and was as well-versed on all betrothals, weddings, births, and court news as anyone could be who had been out of society for five years.

Mrs. Tottle entered with the roasted chicken and dish of fresh peas, followed by Tottle with the wine. The guest agreed that a glass would be very welcome. Tottle winked at his wife as he lovingly uncorked the dusty bottle and poured. Ursula took a sip at once to steady her nerves, and then smiled approvingly at her host.

"You have another guest for the night?" she could not resist asking.

"Yes, indeed, a grand gennleman from Lunnon he be. But don't you worry yourself none, my lady, for I've put him down to his dinner in the taproom, so he won't come bothering you. He's off again in the morning," Tottle added regretfully.

"I thought I heard a carriage before."

"No, that not be hissen. He rode in on a great raking black beast. Fine a horse as ever I seed."

"Come along, Tottle," his wife said when she saw that Ursula had nothing further to say. "Let my lady have her dinner in peace."

Ursula had her dinner, and her wine. Each time she thought of the "great gentleman from London" sitting in the taproom having his dinner, she took another sip to calm her fluttering pulses, and quite soon it was all gone. She regretted having assured Tottle that she never had more than one glass.

Would *he* come in again? No, of course he would not. What could interest him in a poor little wren of a creature such as herself, who could not even keep her countenance when she met a gentleman unexpectedly? Besides, he had not recognized her. So humiliating. With this thought she gathered up her fan and reticule and went hurriedly up to bed.

Carey helped her to undress and then retired. Ursula climbed between the coarse but sweet-smelling sheets and blew out her candle. A soft glow lit the room from the embers of the fire, and she stared at the coals, thinking it would be very unlikely their paths would cross again, which was just as well, since it was so unsettling and would no doubt keep her awake all night. She then abruptly fell asleep.

She came down to breakfast next morning, dressed for traveling and ravenous. While she made a hearty breakfast she was informed by Mrs. Tottle that the grand gentleman had eaten just as large a meal and set off half an hour ago.

Ursula was grateful to receive this information without having to inquire, also to feel a relief, not unmixed with some regret, that the brief *rencontre* had been just that and now she could forget it and think about the days ahead and her reunion with darling India.

As the carriage rolled along through the brightly sunlit morning, her spirits rose and she began chatting gaily to Carey of the scenery, of how much she was looking forward to her visit, and how nice was the inn they had just left. As yesterday, they stopped at midday to change the horses and take refreshment, and soon went off again.

"It cannot be much farther now. We've come—" Ursula began, when suddenly there was a shout and the carriage came abruptly to a halt, with much rearing and snorting from the horses, and curses as the coachman sawed at the reins. Ursula let down the window and leaned out. "What is it?" she called. "What . . . ? Oh, dear heaven!"

She threw open the door and jumped down and began running up the road. She saw a large black horse lying on its side, which raised its head to whinny pitifully as she ran past to the huddled mass that lay very still some yards farther on. There was a great deal of blood, indeed his face was covered with it, from a great gash across his right temple. She fell to her knees beside him, fumbling in her pocket for her handkerchief, which she pressed against the wound to stanch the flow. Carey flopped down beside her breathlessly.

"Laws, m'lady, whatever—"

"Quick, Carey, tear a strip from my petticoat to make a larger pad, and something to bind it."

"Tear a strip . . . ? What . . . ? Why . . . ?"

"Oh, never mind. Here, hold this—hard!" She took Carey's hand and pressed it to the handkerchief. She then tore the strip from her petticoat, noticing as she did so the coachman and footman pausing to examine the horse. "Never mind the horse now," she cried. "Fetch me the brandy flask from the small case inside the carriage and see if you can find some water."

She tore off a piece of her strip and folded it into a thick pad, removed her blood-soaked handkerchief, and replaced it with the pad, binding it into place with what was left of the strip. The coachman came lumbering up with the brandy flask, and she raised the unconscious man's head as he tried to force some of the brandy into his mouth. It only ran out the sides, mixing horridly with the blood.

"Never mind, Jakes, he can't take it now. See if you can discover if he has broken any bones."

Very gingerly Jakes flexed the arms and legs. "Nothin' visibly, m'lady, but that horse has broke his left fore and should be put out of his misery."

"Yes. Oh, Williams, you found some water!"

"Little brook just into the trees there on the right."

"How clever of you," she murmured as she tore off another strip of her petticoat and soaked it in the hatful of water Williams held for her. "While I clean him up, Jakes, do you go and do as you must about that poor beast. Then come back, and we'll get the gentleman into the carriage."

"Why, what you think to do with him, m'lady?" Jakes asked.

"Well, we cannot leave him in the road, so we must take him with us. How far is it to Swan Court, would you say?"

"No more than five miles now, m'lady."

"Then we must take Lord Henry there."

"Why, do you know this gentleman, m'lady?" Carey asked in astonishment.

"Yes, he is Lord Henry Somerton. I met him in London many years ago."

"Well, I vow, of all strange things."

"Yes, but please let us move quickly now."

Jakes and Williams went off, and in a moment came the pistol blast and then they were back.

"Jakes, do you and Williams take him up as carefully as you can, and, Carey, you walk beside to support his head. Williams, I am sorry, but I must keep your hatful of water to bathe Lord Henry's face as we go. I will go ahead and get into the carriage, and you will lift him in with his head in my lap. Carey, you will sponge his face from time to time and try again to get some brandy down him. You must drive very slowly, Jakes."

These arrangements were carried out, and soon they were on their way again, at a funereal place. It was some time before Ursula's nerves steadied enough to allow any thought to her position. She was unaware that there was a smear of blood on her forehead where she had pushed back a straying hair, that the front of her gown was filthy from kneeling in the dirt of the road and was now also bloodstained, but she was aware that she would be arriving very much later than she had written India to expect her, and in a most peculiar manner. She only hoped India had no other guests.

Then, for some reason she remembered the kitten from that first inn yesterday and her reluctance to foist such a burden upon a friend. How, then, of this burden? Then she brushed the thought aside as of no importance. She knew her friend too well to worry about her reactions.

4

India was expecting Ursula sometime in midafternoon. That was, if there were no unfortunate delays, such as one of the horses' casting a shoe. She was not at all perturbed when it became four o'clock, and not too much when it became five, but by six o'clock she was definitely uneasy. She had sent a boy down to the entrance of the drive with orders to run back quickly to apprise her of his first glimpse of the carriage, and every few moments now she paced out to the top of the steps to see if he was coming.

When, at half-past six, he did appear running up the drive and shouting, she hurried out and down the steps, her happy smile already beaming welcome. It slowly faded as moments passed and no carriage appeared. When it came in sight at last she realized why it had taken so long, for the carriage was moving at something only a little more brisk than a walking pace. Her only thought was that one of the horses had been lamed. She waved energetically, but received no response, saw no eager face emerge from the window. Behind her her mother-in-law had come out to the top of the steps, followed by Crigly and several footmen.

"How very peculiar. Imagine traveling with a footman wearing no hat," the Dowager commented.

The carriage creaked to a halt and the hatless footman leapt down to open the door and let down the steps, but no one instantly appeared in the doorway. India stepped up to the door, her expression of delight changing all at once when

31

her eyes met Ursula's, their blue darkened with anxiety, her
face pale, her smile tremulous and tentative. At the same
instant, India took in the figure disposed on the seat, the
bloodily bandaged head, with, surely, a narrow lace ruffle
incongruously over one eye, reposing in Ursula's lap, and
the abigail holding, improbably, a hat. India's mouth opened,
but before she could speak, Ursula said urgently, "India,
send someone for a doctor at once."

Without questions or hesitation, India called over her
shoulder, "Crigly, send someone for a doctor at once—an
emergency, and he's to come as quickly as possible. Send
a footman for my lord, he's in his gun room. And someone
to tell the housekeeper quickly to make up the bed in the
Blue Room. Carey, step out, if you please . . . What on
earth . . .!" she exclaimed as Carey obediently climbed
down, carefully holding the hat, as one would a basin, which
India could now see was half full of pinkish water and a
blood-soaked cloth. "Oh . . . oh . . . someone please take
. . . oh, thank you . . ." This to Williams, who stepped
forward and silently retrieved his hat. "Crigly, do you . .
.? Oh, Robert, my dear, here you are—an injured man—
would you go around to the other side and take his shoulders,
and, Crigly, come up and take his middle, and you, John,"
beckoning to a footman, "come and take his feet." Not even
Robert stopped to question or exclaim, but all did as she bade
them and moved into their allocated positions with alacrity.
Then, as a well-rehearsed team, they lifted Lord Henry
Somerton, and carefully maneuvering down the carriage
steps, reached the drive with him in a moment.

"Straight up and into bed. I have sent for the doctor,
Robert, if you could get him undressed and into one of your
bedgowns, we shall follow you up in a moment. Now,
Ursula, my darling girl . . ." India helped Ursula down the
carriage steps and embraced her warmly, feeling her friend's
body trembling with a release of emotion too long held in
check.

"Oh, India," Ursula breathed with a little sob.

"Yes, dearest, I know. But now we won't speak of anything. You are to come inside and have something to restore your senses, and then we will go up to the patient."

Ursula started forward eagerly from the arm India had about her waist as she led her up the front steps into the house. "Yes, of course, I must go up at once."

"No, dearest, first you must sit quite quietly for a few moments and have your drink while he is put to bed. Now, sit down, do." India pressed her into a chair. "Lupton, bring some brandy at once," she ordered a footman who had opened the door for them. He bowed and hurried away, and had returned with a tray by the time Ursula had removed her bonnet and her bloodstained York tan gloves.

India poured out the brandy and held it out, but Ursula demurred. "Oh, please, I thank you, but I dislike it so very much."

"I know, love, but it is very effective. Try just a few sips," India coaxed, holding the glass to her lips. Ursula obeyed, taking a sip from the glass as a child would; then she shuddered at the taste, but took the glass into her own hand, sipping away at it as she would a medicine, making a wry face with each taste. However, in a few moments some color had returned to her cheeks. "Enough," she said. "I feel much better. I must go up to him."

"I wonder who he can be?"

"Why, did you not recognize him, India? It is Henry Somerton! Surely you remember him?"

"Good heavens!" India was aghast, for here was the only man, as far as she was aware, who had ever touched Ursula's heart, and it was her belief, though never expressed to Ursula nor expressed by Ursula, that he still held a place there. For a certainty, he had been the reason for her refusal of every offer she had received when she had had her Seasons in London. Of course, she had had very little chance to meet anyone since, immured as she had been with her mother for so long. She had never in all that time mentioned any gentleman's name beyond Lord Batesly, and that with scorn and loathing.

Now, here was Lord Henry Somerton in the house, gravely injured, possibly fatally injured! India felt her heart wrench with pity for her friend. Before she could respond, however, the dowager came in.

"Ah, here you are, my child. I have brought my vinaigrette for you, for I was sure you would be in need of it."

"That is very kind, Mother, but as you can see, Ursula is feeling much more the thing now."

"I brought it for you, my dear," the dowager said reproachfully, "all this shock and excitement has surely upset you, and—"

"Not in the least. I am feeling very well, except for distress about my friend. Oh, I believe you have not met. Ursula, this is Robert's mother."

Ursula rose and dropped a curtsy, to which the dowager nodded condescendingly. "Lady Ursula, I am sure you must want to be shown to your room. There is blood on your face and gown."

She said this in such accusatory tones that Ursula touched her face and looked down at her gown guiltily.

"Good heavens, Mother, what can that matter when a person has been seriously injured? I am sure Ursula never took thought of her appearance at such a time," India retorted spiritedly.

"No, I did not, until this moment. Do forgive me, Lady Swanson, for appearing before you in all my dirt. I will go up and wash my face and hands now, India, if I may. Then I will look in on Lord Henry."

"In his bedroom!" the dowager exclaimed, much scandalized.

"The gentleman is unconscious, Mother, and Robert is there. Come, Ursula."

Carey, happily, had already ordered hot water, and Ursula hastily washed her face and hands, while India waited with a towel. Carey had also laid out a clean gown, but Ursula could not be stayed to change it. Carey threw up her hands in despair, but India only took Ursula's arm and led her to the door of the Blue Room. She knocked softly, and it was answered at once by Robert.

"Ah, there you are! We have him in bed at last, and I was just trying to decide if I should change his bandage. The wound seems to have stopped bleeding."

Ursula went swiftly to the bedside and felt his hands and face, which showed no signs of fever as yet, though his pulse was rapid.

"We must change the bandage. I would rather the doctor were here to do it, but I cannot bear to leave that filthy rag in place. Is there warm water and—?"

"I have ordered everything—it is here."

"Oh, good, then I will just . . ." Gingerly she untied the tightly bound cloth, frivolously lace-edged, then lifted off the stiffened brownish pad. Very gently she washed the wound, then his face. The gash began to ooze blood, but sluggishly now. She formed another thick pad, and holding the edges of the gash together with her fingers, laid the pad over it and pressed it hard as she slipped her fingers out, then gestured to India to wrap a strip of linen tightly over the pad. India did this deftly, and tied a neat knot over his left temple.

There was a sigh of relief from everyone but Lord Somerton, who remained profoundly unconscious. "Can it be good for him to be so long in coming round?" asked Ursula worriedly.

"Whether good or bad, we cannot know," Robert said. "We have tried several times to revive him, but he doesn't respond. I think, since we can do no other, we must simply have patience until the doctor arrives."

India said, "I know, darling, that it seems forever, but truly it has not been twenty minutes since you pulled up at the door. The boy may have reached the doctor by now, almost surely has, but the doctor may be out, or . . . Who knows? In any case, the boy won't return without him, you may be sure. Why do you not come away now and rest?"

"Oh, no, India, I could not, indeed I could not. I am perfectly calm, I assure you. If I could just be allowed to sit here by the bedside . . . and perhaps a cup of coffee."

"Of course you may. We will all have some, and while we wait, maybe you would tell us what happened," India said, nodding to Crigly to fetch up some coffee.

Robert pulled up an upholstered armchair beside the bed and Ursula sat down in it quite suddenly, as though her knees had given way. "Oh," she said softly, and without another sound slumped over the arm of the chair in a faint. India swooped upon her, snatched up the vinaigrette bottle on the bedside table, and waved it under her nose. In less than a moment Ursula straightened up and looked groggily about her. "Good heavens, did I faint? I never did so in my life! It is a very odd feeling."

"Oh, my darling, all this has been too much for you!"

"No, no, India. Good heavens, I have been through much worse with Mama. You know I am strong as an ox. No, it is only the anxiety. He is . . . I . . ." She stopped suddenly, warm color flooding into her pale face.

India smiled. "Yes, of course. Ah, here is the coffee. That will restore you. Now, have some, and then tell us all about how the fair maiden rode to the rescue of the knight in danger."

"Oh, India, it was so dreadful. The poor horse had to be shot! There was this very deep rut, and he broke his leg. And there was Lord Henry, just lying there so still, his face covered with blood—I was sure he was dead! We found this large sharp-edged stone, all bloody, and he had evidently been thrown headfirst upon it."

"But you recognized him at once?"

"Oh, yes," Ursula said simply.

"After so many years, to come upon him like that. You poor darling."

"I had seen him last night—at the inn—only for an instant. He did not recognize me, of course."

India stiffened indignantly at the "of course," and was prepared to make a sharp retort about Henry Somerton, but then thought better of it. The poor child looked so pale and weary.

There was a tap at the door, and Crigly showed in the doctor, who only nodded at his introduction to Ursula, his eye already upon his patient. He brusquely ordered all but Robert to leave the room and went straight to the bedside.

Ursula and India huddled together silently in the hall for what seemed ages before the doctor came out again.

"Well, he is concussed, I would say, but there is no way to tell how serious his condition is while he is unconscious. There is nothing really to be done, except to keep the wound clean and himself warm. He has no fever as yet, so bleeding him would not help. I will come again in the morning to see how he goes on. Good day to you."

5

Ursula spent the rest of that day at her patient's bedside, with Robert and India looking in from time to time with offers to relieve her, but she would not be persuaded. She did relent and allow them to send up a maid to sit with Lord Henry while she came down to dinner, knowing that she was giving her friends trouble and worry to repay them for their kindness. She also consented to allow two maids to watch Lord Henry in shifts through the night, but she had little rest from this, for her terror of his dying with only strangers beside him caused her to jerk from sleep every hour or so. She would then hastily don a robe and tiptoe along the hall to his room, where she would take his pulse and check his forehead for fever.

Her uneasy night showed in her face the next morning, but she refused to acknowledge any weariness. Indeed, she felt none, for she was in much too nervous a state to feel anything beyond anxiety.

The doctor arrived soon after breakfast, accompanied by a large red-faced nurse he had brought along to attend his patient. Ursula protested that she was perfectly capable of nursing him herself, having spent the last five years attending her mother.

"Ah, but your patient was a female, my dear lady. You cannot possibly bathe and change the gentleman, and I doubt you are strong enough to move him when the sheets must be changed, eh?"

The nurse simpered and looked pleased at this rebuke, and

Ursula blushed and subsided, but took an instant dislike to the nurse, who proved to be bossy and clearly of the opinion that Ursula's presence in the sickroom was an intrusion. Ursula spent another uneasy night and day.

On the third night, exhaustion overcame her at last, and by midnight she had fallen into a deep sleep. It seemed only a moment later that Carey woke her with clanking cans of hot water, which she was pouring into a bath set before the fire.

"Oh, Carey, just when I had fallen asleep," she protested sleepily.

"Yes, my lady, but breakfast will be served soon, and you must have your bath. Why, it has been three days! You've still the dust of the road on you."

After her long sleep and her bath, Ursula, in a pale blue flounced muslin, went down to breakfast feeling very much refreshed. She had tapped at Lord Henry's door, but the nurse had refused her admittance, saying she was just bathing his lordship.

India jumped up from the breakfast table to greet her guest with a warm embrace. "There, now, how pretty you look. I'm so glad you were able to sleep at last—not that I blame you in the least for wanting to nurse him. When one rescues a stranger . . . well, he is not exactly a stranger, of course, but almost, if you know what I mean . . . well, one would want to make sure he is receiving every attention—one feels so responsible, do you see? Here, sit down now, and you must eat a very large breakfast."

Robert, who had risen at her entrance, now came around to kiss Ursula's cheek and pull back her chair. Before she sat down, Ursula turned to drop a curtsy to the dowager, who nodded in reply, not halting her business of cutting into the steak set before her.

"I recommend this beef to your notice, Lady Ursula," she said. "It is very strengthening, and I feel sure after all your troubles, you can use some hearty fare."

"How very kind of you, Lady Swanson, but I have never been able to face red meat in the morning," Ursula murmured, accepting some baked eggs being offered her by the manservant.

"Hmph! I cannot approve of such die-away airs as you young girls profess these days. In my day young girls were expected to eat well and keep up their strength as a preventive to illness."

"Oh, I am never ill," Ursula said.

"No wonder if you were, after coming upon such a sight in the roads. Really, these gentleman stravaging about on great brutes of horses, never looking where they are going, creating such horrors! Served him right if no one had come along to save him from his own folly."

"Oh, Mama, surely you cannot mean that?" Robert protested mildly.

"Certainly I do! Why, a delicately nurtured female might be sent into fits or start a brain fever upon seeing such a sight. Such a careless rider has no right to impose so upon decent people."

"But surely decent people should come to the aid of anyone in distress, Lady Swanson?"

The dowager drew herself up affrontedly. "I feel sure that a young woman of your breeding could not mean to be disrespectful to her elders, Lady Ursula."

"I meant no disrespect, but if you found it so, I am sure I beg your pardon."

"Of course, my child, I am sure your nerves must still be every which way from your ordeal. After all, it is very . . . *outré* to be forced to arrive as a guest accompanied by a bloodstained and unconscious man. Not at all the sort of thing one expects."

"Good heavens, Mama, you make it sound as though Ursula is to blame somehow," Robert laughed.

The dowager laid her knife and fork slowly across her plate, folded her napkin carefully and laid it upon the table, and rose. "I see I am to be taken up sharply for my every word this morning. You will excuse me, I am sure." She made her way with stately dignity out the door.

"Oh, dear, I am so sorry if I—" Ursula began contritely.

"Pooh! Pay no attention at all. Mother always takes the other side, no matter what the discussion may be. Does she not, Robert?"

"Always," he replied succinctly.

"You see? Now, eat up your breakfast, and we are going out for a nice walk."

"Oh, India, I could not. I must go up and—"

"No, you must not! The nurse will be sure to call us at once if there is any change, and the doctor won't be here for an hour. You have not put a foot out the door for three days. You need air and exercise, and I mean to see you have it!"

"Darling India, you are so good to me. Robert, should we not notify some member of his family? I mean, he might not . . ." She could not bring herself to finish the sentence.

"Recover?" Robert said. "Of course he will. It is only a knock on the head, you know. As for his family, I wrote to his sister yesterday. She is married to some Scots lord up in the Highlands. There is a younger brother, but he is in India with his regiment. His parents are both dead, as you probably know."

"How clever you are to have thought of it so quickly. I confess I only thought of it just now."

"You have been somewhat preoccupied," India said dryly. "Come along now and fetch your bonnet."

Ursula did as she was told. She hesitated outside Lord Henry's door, but hadn't the courage to face the nurse again, and went, somewhat reluctantly, down the stairs. After only a few moments in the fresh air, however, she felt some of the weight of her anxiety lift at the beauty of the early-summer morning, the air still moist with the dew being pulled up by the sun, and with it the delicate scent of grass and flowers.

Arm in arm, the two women walked through shrubberies, rose gardens, herb gardens, and at last into a small copse, hazed with color by a riotous growth of bluebells.

Ursula stopped, enchanted. "Oh, India!" she breathed softly.

"I know. It is my favorite place at this time of the year. It is like a fairyland, is it not? Shall we sit for a while? Robert had a bench put in for me over there under that tree."

They sat down and presently began to talk, as two old and very close friends can, as though there had been no separation between them, of all the things they could say to no other. Ursula spoke openly of the frustration and boredom of those lonely years tending her mother, of her mother's difficult temperament and unkindness. India unburdened herself of some of her feelings about her mother-in-law's meddling ways that caused her resentment she tried not to express, since, after all, it was her dear Robert's mother, and grandmother of the child to come.

After a time they strolled back toward the house, crossing the lawns and circling the house to the front to see if the doctor had arrived. There was no carriage standing there, but one was approaching as they came up.

"Oh, dear heavens, that is not Dr. Forsythe, it is the Rochdale carriage and pair. I hope you will not mind, dearest, they are really lovely girls and they will not stay long."

"Mind! That your neighbors come calling? Heavens, India, what must you think of me to say such a thing?"

"Well, in the ordinary way I would not, but just now, when you are so tired and distracted . . ."

"Nonsense, my love. I shall like meeting your neighbors."

There was no time to say more, for the carriage drew up before them. In a moment the door was opened, the steps were let down, and a young gentleman stepped forth, bowed, and then turned back to hand out two young girls, who threw themselves upon India with rapturous cries to embrace and kiss her.

India disentangled herself, laughing, and turned to Ursula. "Allow me to present Miss Rochdale and Miss Anne Rochdale. Lady Ursula Liddiard."

They bobbed a curtsy each and smiled shyly. They were very alike, with no more than a year between them, and very young, no more than fifteen and sixteen. They were blonds with brown, twinkling eyes and pert little noses.

"Oh, Lady Swanson, here is our brother, Tarquin, back from the West Indies at last," Miss Rochdale exclaimed, gazing adoringly at her brother.

"Sir Tarquin, this is a pleasant surprise," India said, holding out her hand. He bowed over it to kiss her fingertips.

"No greater than my pleasure to be here, Lady Swanson. My sisters' letters have been so filled with your praises that I took the first opportunity to meet you. I hope you will not mind my accompanying them without any notice."

Here was the original die from which the two lesser coins had been struck, their print less firm and clear than the first. The sisters, pretty as they were, paled to insignificance beside him. His tight gold curls fitted his head like a cap, glinting in the sunlight, the brown eyes very fine and bold, the bones of his face and the shape of his mouth firm and clear-cut, his fairness enhanced by a skin tanned from the West Indian sun. He was a most handsome man, indeed.

He turned with an expectant smile to Ursula, and India presented him to her. Her hand also was kissed firmly, and then he raised his smiling face to her. She lowered her gaze to the tops of her shoes before the intensity of the look he gave her.

India led them all into the drawing room, and while they were settling, Miss Rochdale began explaining eagerly that they had been looking forward to Lady Ursula's visit, having heard so much of her from dear Lady Swanson. This speech was interrupted by Miss Anne to express their sympathy for her recent loss. Ursula managed to smile and look grave where appropriate, but her whole being was concentrated on listening for the sound of the doctor's carriage.

Instead she heard a firm tread in the hall that she at once recognized and that caused her skin to cringe in dread. She had had her share of disagreeable old ladies.

The dowager flung open the door and advanced confidently into the room, then feigned surprise. "Why, India, my dear, I was unaware we had guests," she said chidingly. "I will order some refreshment for them."

"I have already done so, Mother. Allow me to present Sir Tarquin Rochdale to you."

The old lady extended her hand graciously and smiled somewhat coquettishly as he bent over it. The Rochdale sisters came to make their curtsies. The dowager seated herself and took over the conversation. India allowed this for about ten minutes before firmly taking over again in a brief pause while the dowager stopped to take a sip of wine, and began telling the Rochdales of Ursula's adventure, eliciting horrified cries from the young ladies. Ursula sat quietly, aching to excuse herself and try once more to gain entrance to the sickroom, just to check for herself that he still lived, but she had not enough courage to conduct herself in such a singular way as to cause India embarrassment before her neighbors. She would also have liked to escape the gaze of Sir Tarquin, whose fine brown eyes seemed to press upon her insistently, almost forcing her to raise her eyes from time to time, much as she did not want to. Not the least part of her discomfort was her awareness of the dowager's sharp eyes taking in the situation fully.

At last she was rewarded for her patience by the sound of a carriage on the drive, and she turned eagerly to the window. "Oh, that surely must be the doctor at last!" she exclaimed involuntarily.

Miss Rochdale rose at once, saying they must take themselves from underfoot. Her brother and sister rose also, and they left in a flurry of cheek kissing between the ladies and further hand kissing from Sir Tarquin. As soon as they were alone in the drawing room, Ursula moved over to sit beside India, her groping hand clasped at once by India's sympathetic one.

The dowager, with an arch smile, said, "Well, well, Lady Ursula, that was a complete *coup de foudre* if ever I saw one. I must congratulate you."

Ursula jerked around toward her, her eyes wide, startled and apprehensive. "C-congratulate? I do not understand."

"Pho, pho, pho, no missish airs, if you please," retorted the dowager, wagging her finger and smiling.

"Mother, what on earth are you talking about?" India demanded, patience barely held in check.

"Why, Lady Ursula's conquest. Surely you cannot mean to say you did not notice? Why, he could not take his eyes from her."

Ursula felt the color flood into her face, but she drew herself up and said calmly, "I hope you will not think me rude, Lady Swanson, if I say that you refine too much on what was merely curiosity."

Before the dowager could reply, there was the sound of the doctor's footsteps on the stairs, and both India and Ursula rose and swiftly rushed out into the hall to confront him.

He assured them that though still unconscious, Lord Henry's heart and pulse were strong and steady, and he, the doctor, had no fears. The nurse must be relieved for some hours tonight, but he felt sure Lady Swanson would make some suitable arrangement with her staff. He asked to be summoned at once if there was any change, otherwise he would call again in the morning, and he bade them a brisk good day and was gone in a moment.

"I will relieve the nurse," Ursula said firmly.

"Oh, my dear," India began, ready to protest ag...
another sleepless night for her friend, but seeing the look
on Ursula's face, she changed her mind. "Yes, dearest, of
course you will."

It was arranged that Ursula would take the first watch after
dinner and would be relieved by the nurse at two in the
morning. She ate her dinner, too aware of the dowager's
disapproving eye upon her to allow herself to show how eager
she was to be gone to her duties, but the food had no taste
to her and had to be forced down. The meal seemed endless,
course after course coming on relentlessly. She talked and
smiled and told herself that it must all be over at last and
that she owed it to India and Robert to be an entertaining
guest for once and not a burden who must be fussed over.

She was released at last and was back in the sickroom,
listening meekly to all the nurse's instructions, nodding and
serious. When the door closed at last behind the formidable
back, Ursula breathed a sigh of relief and pulled a chair up
to the bedside.

She stared into the still, closed-off face, and her hand went
out impulsively to smooth back the dark curls on his
forehead. Then she drew her hand back. I have no right,
she thought, and somehow it is too much an invasion of his
privacy to touch him when he cannot protest if he does not
like it.

She folded her hands in her lap and sat back in the chair,
reminded of so many watchful nights at her mother's bedside.
But then, of course, she had dreaded the thought of her
mother waking, fretful and complaining, or worse, moaning
in pain. She rose abruptly to scatter those bad memories and
walked about the room, then stood for a time at the window
looking out into the dark garden. Then she resolutely returned
to her chair and took up the book she had provided herself
with, the newest novel by Miss Austen. She tried to immerse
herself in it, but even Miss Austen could not hold her tonight.

After she had stared unseeingly at the page for some time, the print blurred and her lids began to droop. Then, very faintly, a whisper of sound pierced the silence and her eyes flew open.

Lord Henry's head, all these days a profile straight up to the ceiling, was turned away on the pillow. She felt her heart fluttering rapidly, and reached out for his wrist to check his pulse, and as she held it, his head came slowly around toward her. He lay there quietly for a moment, then even more slowly his eyes opened, only inches from her own as she bent toward him.

He stared at her for a long moment and then said, quite clearly, "So they *are* such a color. So very blue, like dark sapphires."

Then, with a contented sigh, his eyes closed and he fell asleep again, but now the hand she had kept upon his wrist was firmly enclosed within his own.

6

Though Ursula knew that of course she must report to the nurse that Lord Henry had moved and spoken during the past hour, she did not think she could tell her what he had said. For one thing, she was not entirely sure those words were meant as she had interpreted them. Even the thought of this made her blush, for she now saw that they could have meant any of a half-dozen things, none of them connected with her or the color of her eyes.

As soon as the first intimation of this had entered her mind, she had hurriedly withdrawn the hand she had left in his clasp. This had not wakened him, for the deep sleep he had fallen into had some time before loosened his clasp. Thank heaven she had done so, for the nurse entered the room abruptly and marched starchily across to the bed.

"He has moved," she said accusingly.

"Y-yes. Yes, he has. About a half-hour ago he stirred and then opened his eyes and spoke."

"What did he say?"

"Oh, he . . . well . . . something about blue and . . . er . . . sapphires," Ursula stuttered.

"Did he sound delirious . . . muttering?"

"Oh, no. He spoke quite coherently. Just the one sentence. He has no fever."

"No, I see. Very well. I will take over now. Good night . . . my lady," she added with evident reluctance.

Though Ursula was up so late, it was some time before

her mind settled enough to allow her to fall asleep, but she woke feeling both refreshed and excited, as though the day held promise of some pleasure. She remembered when, a very little girl, she had felt this way on birthday mornings when she first woke.

She remembered the night before and leapt out of bed, rang for her abigail, and began to wash before her morning chocolate could be brought to her. On her way down to breakfast, she tapped softly at Lord Henry's door. The nurse was very unforthcoming.

"No . . . my lady, he hasn't stirred again, and I won't have him disturbed till he's had his sleep out."

"Naturally, I would not dream of doing so," Ursula returned with as much dignity as she could muster after such a rude response. She pulled herself up as tall as possible and turned to proceed in a stately way down the stairs. Really, she thought, that woman is insufferable.

"Well, dearest, here you are! I hope you are not exhausted from your long vigil," India exclaimed as her friend entered the breakfast room.

"No, no, not the least in the world. Good morning, Lady Swanson, good morning, Robert. Just think, he woke last night, for just a moment, and spoke!"

"What did he say?" India asked excitedly.

"Oh, nothing that made any sense."

"But what?" India persisted.

"Oh, darling, I don't exactly recall. Something about colors—blue, sapphire, something like that." Ursula felt a betraying warmth in her cheeks and took a bite of toast as nonchalantly as possible.

"Delirious, no doubt," the dowager said.

"Well, perhaps, though he had no fever and his pulse was normal."

"Could be a brain fever, nevertheless, brought on by the shock," the dowager said.

"Oh, dear, I do hope not," Ursula cried, the color draining from her cheeks.

"Pooh! I do not think so in the least," India said rallyingly. "Do you, Robert?"

"I am not a doctor, my dear, any more than are you. Nor is Mama. Why don't we wait until someone who is can see him and give us his opinion?"

"Hmph! All very well, my son, but when a man begins to rave—" the dowager began.

"Oh, no," Ursula protested. "Pray forgive me for interrupting you, madam, but he did not rave in the least. He spoke quite quietly, quite clearly, then went to sleep."

"Well, you said before that his speech made no sense, young woman. I am only going upon your word."

"I only meant his words made no sense to me."

"But they were comprehensible words? Not babbling?" the dowager demanded in a hectoring way.

"Certainly he was not babbling!"

"Then perhaps it would reassure all of us if you would repeat them as clearly as he spoke them," the Dowager said with tart triumph.

"Oh, Mama, what does it matter what he said? It cannot pertain to anything we know of," Robert said impatiently.

"Very well, my son, if you will have it so," the dowager replied huffily, and turned back to her letters. After a moment she exclaimed, "Well, well, here is welcome news indeed! Blanche writes proposing herself for a visit. She was to go to the Prestons, but one of the children has chickenpox, so she wonders if she might come here. I shall write at once to assure her she will be most welcome."

Robert, also absorbed in his letters, looked up at this. "What do you say? Who is welcome?"

"Blanche Vernon, your cousin. My niece."

"I am aware of the relationship, Mama, but it does not make me any more eager to see her."

"Why, Robert, how can you? You know how fond Blanche has always been of you. Surely you will welcome the opportunity of a visit from her after so long?"

"Not necessarily." Then, seeing by his mother's expression that she would continue to press for the visit, he relented. "Oh, very well, I suppose she must come—but only if India will not mind."

The dowager's eyebrows rose at this, as if to question what difference India's opinion could possibly make after her own had been expressed.

Though India would have preferred the visit at any other time, she thought the issue too small to make a protest. "Why, of course she is welcome, Mother, if you like to have her."

Later she confided to Ursula that Robert had been plagued by the dowager for years before he married to make a match with his cousin, saying that she and her sister had planned it when Robert and Blanche were but babies. Robert, however, had disliked Blanche from the time he was able to make distinctions between good people and bad people, saying his cousin told lies about him and was an out-and-out sneaksby when they were children and had done everything possible to get him into trouble. What India did not confide was that Blanche made such a dead set at every eligible man who came her way that she did not like to have her in the house while Lord Henry was here. India wondered whether Ursula would mind Blanche flirting with Lord Henry. She could not decide whether Ursula still had some feeling for him. The only basis she had for imagining that it might be so was girlish confidences exchanged after a ball during the year of Ursula's come-out, when she had confessed that Lord Henry represented her *beau ideal*. She had never said any more about him than that, but India had noticed after that the way Ursula's eyes had, very discreetly, followed that gentleman's progress if he were in the room, and how, though she had attended all the parties and danced every dance and received several proposals, she had never, even for a moment, shown the least evidence of interest in any other man.

Though Ursula never made any other confidences concerning Lord Henry, nor, during the past five years, referred to him in her letters, India was not convinced that her friend had not conceived an unrequited passion for the man. She could not be very sure, for though Ursula was certainly worried about Lord Henry, it was no more than India herself would have shown if she had rescued a dangerously injured man, known or unknown, and he lay, for all anyone yet knew, at death's door. In reviewing all she knew of the business, India found that it was very flimsy evidence, based on one clear statement of attraction by an eighteen-year-old girl and little else beyond India's own youthful romanticism.

Indeed, Ursula herself could not have given an account of her feelings about the gentleman. She had stated truthfully her feelings about him to India all those years ago, but even then she had not been in love with him. Young as she was at the time, she would not have been so foolish as to give her heart away to anyone solely because of his handsome face and figure. She had watched out for him at parties and balls, but she had never been asked by him to stand up for a dance, so she had never had a chance to know him. He had been introduced to her at one point, and afterward he had bowed to her if he noticed her, but they had had no conversation together. At the end of that Season she remained heart whole, and during her second Season he was much less in evidence and she thought very little about him. Then the long barren years of nursing her mother all but erased him from her mind. She did often think of those two lovely Seasons of gaiety, but since he had never been within her reach, it was not of him, but of the opportunities spurned at the time, which could have spared her the tedious loneliness she had endured, for who knew but that she might have learned to love one of those gentlemen if she had not felt that love must come upon the instant, like a flash of lightning? She might now have a devoted husband and a nursery full of children, instead of this arid old-maidenly dust of emptiness in her soul. For despite her brave words to her brother, she felt that time had passed her by and left her upon the shelf.

Seeing Lord Henry at that inn had of course called to mind her youthful fancies, but more than anything it had been a humiliating experience for her, for he had not recognized her. She flushed every time she remembered this, even now after she had found him in the road and had brought him here, after sitting beside his bed for so many hours, even after his moment of consciousness last night, when he had held her hand. That had meant nothing at all, it had only embarrassed her. She would have traded those moments gladly for just one moment at that inn when he might have said, "Why, it is Lady Ursula Liddiard, is it not?"

That would have given her a solid feeling of being something more than a nonentity. She hated minding so much, and told herself that after their very few casual encounters in London five years ago he could not be blamed for not knowing her, but still she minded. Not for any romantic notions cherished in her breast all these years, but simply for her own self-esteem.

Her worry for him these past days had been the horror of his possibly dying among strangers, not even aware that an old acquaintance was by him to give him comfort in his last moments, though how much comfort he might derive from an unremembered casual acquaintance she was unable to measure.

Walking out in the shrubbery with India after breakfast, she confessed to her how very uncongenial she found the nurse.

"Yes, she is a horror," India agreed. "Ah, here is the doctor coming now. If he finds our patient to be recovering, perhaps we can ask him to take the woman away. You and I could surely tend him, and Robert's valet would willingly assist in his bathing and changing.''

When the doctor came down from seeing his patient, he found the two ladies awaiting him and immediately questioned Ursula on the brief awakening of the night before. Ursula told him of it word for word.

"And what was his manner as he spoke, would you say, my lady?''

"Why, rather as if he were answering a question he had been pondering. Musing, in a way, it seemed,'' Ursula said, so intent on helping the doctor she forgot to be self-conscious about the content of the words.

"Something he was thinking about just before he was thrown and lost consciousness, I should think. Well, I believe we are safely out of the woods. He will have more frequent and longer periods of awareness now. Of course, he must be kept quite quiet for the next week, but then, I imagine, he will be clamoring to get back on a horse.''

"In a week! Oh, surely not, Doctor?'' India exclaimed.

"Oh, yes, I should not be in the least surprised. A very healthy, well-set-up young man like that will be hard to keep quiet for long.''

"If his recovery is assured now, perhaps it will not be necessary to keep the nurse any longer. I am sure that between Lady Swanson and myself, and Lord Swanson's valet, we could care for him,'' Ursula said.

"Ah, you have not taken to Mrs. Graves, I see. She has an unfortunate manner, but she is very reliable. However, let us give it another day before we make the decision, eh?''

He rose, bowed, and went away in a great bustle. Ursula turned to India and hugged her impulsively. "Oh, what a great relief to know all will be well. It is like a great oppressive burden lifted from one's shoulders, isn't it? Now we can really settle down to our visit.''

India thought she could not imagine a less loverlike declaration than this, and realized she had been wrong in her imaginings about the state of Ursula's heart. There had been no years of nursing a flame, as she had thought. She knew herself for a romantic and knew as well that her friend had ever been the opposite: practical and down-to-earth, she would never have allowed herself to behave so.

India was glad, of course, to know that Ursula had not suffered from disappointed love all these years; nevertheless she sighed a little. Before they could leave the hall after their consultation with the doctor, there was a rap of the knocker and Crigly turned again to the door.

On the step was Sir Tarquin Rochdale. He removed his hat and made a sweeping bow, which revealed, behind him, his two sisters mounted and a groom holding Sir Tarquin's horse.

"Good morning, fair ladies. I hope you will forgive us if our early call is inopportune, but my sisters and I are off for a ride, and they would insist upon stopping on the chance that Lady Ursula might be persuaded to join us—and of course your own self, dear Lady Swanson," he added hastily.

"Oh, I thank you, but I could not," India said with a laugh, "but I think you should go, Ursula."

"Oh, no . . . no, I . . . I . . ." Ursula protested.

"Nonsense, my dear, nothing could be better for you, after being cooped up here for so many days."

"Oh, I do not think I should leave—" Ursula began.

India interrupted. "Darling one, allow me to persuade you. I would feel so much better if you would take some exercise." She pleaded so earnestly that Ursula felt it would be churlish to continue to refuse. Apart from that, India might be glad to be relieved of the responsibility for her guest's entertainment for an hour or so. She relented graciously and went away to change into her habit.

When she came down again, the young ladies, who had

dismounted, were hanging, one on each side, upon India's arms and gazing up at her adoringly. India had ordered her own mare saddled and brought around, and Sir Tarquin threw Ursula up into the saddle deftly and then turned to help his sisters to remount before mounting himself.

They trotted off down the drive, India waving them goodbye, and, as it turned out, she had been right to insist on the ride, for Ursula gloried in the air and movement, and she realized how much her body craved exercise. Also, she found Sir Tarquin an enlivening companion, with funny stories of his West Indian visit and very subtle compliments, which she could appreciate without feeling abashed. The weight of his glances was lighter today, convincing her that it was truly only curiosity that had caused him to stare at her so disconcertingly the first time they met.

All in all, she found him an amusing companion, and then, he was so very good to look upon. She did not hesitate to agree when he asked if they might hope to have her company for a ride on the following day.

7

When she entered the house, Ursula came face-to-face with the dowager, just emerging from the dining room, where she had been attempting to rearrange a large epergne of flowers India had arranged and placed upon the table not an hour before. That the dowager had not succeeded in doing anything more than make the arrangement look as though someone had stood some distance away and thrown the flowers into the epergne did not disturb her in the least. All of her attempts to better India's flower arrangements were abortive, but she managed to blind herself to her straggling achievements, convincing herself that she had been successful. The servants always came and carried them away to be corrected, and though in one part of her mind she was aware of it, this also she had blinded herself to.

Now she halted and clasped her hands dramatically against her chest. "My dear child! How very rosy and glowing you look. I fear Sir Tarquin has been very naughty."

"Naughty?"

"Oh, you know these gentlemen, they do like to turn an innocent girl's head with their high-flown compliments. It only succeeds in giving girls wrong ideas. They never mean it, the gentlemen, it is only their naughty ways."

"If Sir Tarquin paid me any 'high-flown' compliments," Ursula said in a voice tight with anger, "I am afraid they sailed harmlessly over my head."

"Oh, hoity-toity! I can see I was right. However, I am

sure you are too sensible at your age not to be grateful for
a little warning from someone old enough to stand in place
of a mother to you. You must always feel free to come to
me for advice now that your own dear mother is not by you
any longer."

"Thank you," Ursula said tersely. "Now, if you will
excuse me, I must change."

She turned and ran swiftly up the stairs, where she met
India in the hall. Seeing Ursula's high color and stormy eyes,
India led her into the drawing room and closed the door.

"What is it, darling? Has something happened?"

"No, no. It was only . . . oh, nothing important, really."

"Now, Ursula, you cannot be looking so angry and tell
me it is nothing important. Surely you can confide in me,"
she coaxed.

"It was just that . . . oh, dear, it all sounds so petty. It
was only the dowager. She met me as I was coming in and
insinuated that Sir Tarquin had been turning my head with
compliments and . . . oh, dear heart, please don't ask me
to go on. It all seems so silly now."

"Not silly," India said, patting her hand, "and most
annoying for you. I know so well how she would do it. For
my sake, I hope you can manage to ingore those things she
says. She cannot seem to help herself, you see. I am so sorry
you have been upset."

She looked so abject that Ursula's anger dissipated
instantly. She threw her arms about her friend and hugged
her warmly. "You are not to give it another thought. I shall
pretend, in future, that I haven't heard her and just smile
enigmatically. That should give her something to think
about."

India laughed and looked relieved. "Thank you, my love,
I knew you would understand. I . . . Where did you see her?"
she interrupted herself suddenly.

"In the dining-room doorway."

"Oh, for heaven's sake!" India said, looking distinctly annoyed. "She will have been messing about with my flowers for the dinner table, and it took me nearly half an hour to get them the way I wanted them. She will do it, though she must surely know she has no gift for it at all. Now I shall have to go down and do it all over."

"How can you be sure she won't just do it again?"

"I shall tell the footman not to take them in until just before dinner." Ursula laughed. "Yes, you see, I have had to become very sly and cunning to outwit her."

"Never mind, dear one, one must cope in the best way one can. How is our patient?"

"I saw the nurse after you were gone, and she reports he is resting comfortably. Shall we go and see for ourselves?"

"Perhaps I should change first and wash my face and hands."

"Then I will go and see about my poor flowers. I will come for you when I have finished."

When she tapped and was bidden to enter Ursula's room twenty-five minutes later, Ursula was seated before her dressing table while Carey brushed her hair into a neat little knot on top of her head and arranged several ringlets before each ear. She had changed into a deep orange muslin made up high in the neck.

"Oh, how pretty you look. Such color in your cheeks. I was right, you see. You did need exercise. I hope he will come every day to take you out."

"I cannot answer for every day, but tomorrow at least he has requested it and I have agreed," Ursula replied demurely.

"Ah, you liked him! I am so glad, for I am very fond of his sisters and thought he was charming."

"Yes, he seems nice. Now, shall we brave the lioness in her den?"

"My den, my dear, no matter what she may believe," India replied resolutely.

Hand in hand they went down the hall to the Blue Room, where India rapped briefly. The door was opened after a moment by the nurse, who said only, "Yes?"

"We have come to see our patient," India said. "Is he awake?"

"Yes, but—"

"You are not bathing him?"

"No, but—"

"Then we will see him," India said decisively, sweeping forward, pulling Ursula after her, and forcing the nurse to step aside. India went straight across to the bed, where Lord Henry, roused by the voices, had turned his head to the door. Ursula hung back somewhat shyly.

"Well, sir. I hope we find you feeling more the thing today?" India said.

"Yes, I thank you . . . er . . ." Lord Henry said, his voice still weak.

"You are wondering who I might be, no doubt. I am your hostess, Lord Henry, India Youngreaves. You are at Swan Court in Sussex."

"Youngreaves? Would that be Robert?"

"The very one."

"And you know who I am?" He sounded puzzled.

"Yes, because you were rescued and recognized by my dear friend who brought you here when she found you unconscious on the road," India said, pulling Ursula forward. "Lady Ursula Liddiard."

He looked at Ursula for a long moment, then said, "Ah, yes," in a satisfied way.

The nurse here thrust herself forward importantly. "I really must protest, Lady Swanson. His lordship is still very weak and—"

India conceded at once. "Yes, you are right. We must not tire you, Lord Henry."

"But you will come back?" he asked anxiously.

"Of course we shall, every day, until you are well enough to come down and join us."

He turned to Ursula and she nodded and smiled, and then they went away, both their hearts lighter with relief. True, he was very pale and his voice had no strength in it at all, but he was conscious at last and seemed to have his wits about him, and there was no fever.

The doctor relieved them of the doughty Mrs. Graves the next day, and Lord Swanson's valet, Ursula, India, and the housekeeper took over. Every day after her ride, Ursula went with India to visit Lord Henry, and gradually his story was unfolded to him. He requested that a note be sent to Mr. Lawrence Poynton at Brook House, Sussex, to inform him of what had happened to cause Lord Henry not to appear for his arranged visit and to ask that his own valet, no doubt waiting there for him, post off to Swan Court at once.

He then began to thank Ursula so earnestly that she became abashed and offered many disclaimers of having done anything extraordinary. But despite her obvious embarrassment, he continued to refer to her courage as often as before.

Robert visited him in the afternoons for a short time, and that was the extent of visitors, on orders from the doctor, who had been acquainted with the dowager for some years and was particularly anxious that his patient not be subjected to any visits from her while he was lying helpless in bed.

The dowager continued to persecute Ursula with arch remarks or meaningfully raised eyebrows if they encountered each other before or after Ursula's rides with Sir Tarquin. Ursula would only smile and turn away, causing the dowager some momentary puzzlement but no real change in attitude. She had decided that Ursula must marry Sir Tarquin. It would be a most suitable match, for Sir Tarquin must surely be in need of a wife and had seemed to show a definite partiality for her. He, moreover, was certainly as high as Lady Ursula could hope to look, not being in the first flush of youth, nor an heiress, nor an acknowledged beauty.

Their for the most part pleasant routine was interrupted by the advent of Miss Blanche Vernon, the dowager's niece. She was announced one morning as they all sat at breakfast, and followed swiftly upon Crigly's heels when he came to announce her.

"My dearest Blanche," the dowager cried, rising eagerly and bustling around the table to embrace her. India also rose to salute her with a kiss on the cheek. Robert merely rose, bowed, and said, " 'Morning, Blanche," before continuing with his breakfast. India then introduced Ursula.

Blanche surveyed Ursula coolly and bowed in acknowledgment before allowing herself to be led to a seat at the table, where a place had hastily been set for her by a footman. She was served with coffee and toast and proceeded to entertain them with the story of her bad fortune in her visit to the Prestons, of how careless it was of them to allow their offspring to contact chickenpox, of how bad the roads had been and how tedious the journey.

She was a tall, slim blond with finely cut features, excellent complexion, and pale green eyes. She was handsome and self-centered, with an exaggerated notion of her beauty and worth, which remained undaunted at the age of six-and-twenty with no suitor in sight. She came from a good but undistinguished family residing in Northumberland. She spent her time in visiting friends in London during the Season and their country homes out of season. Most of her waking hours were spent mapping out her campaign to inveigle these invitations. The rest were spent on plans to bring one of the various unattached gentlemen she met on her peregrinations around the country to come up to scratch, so far with a marked lack of success.

She now ordered baked eggs, sipped her coffee, and drawled, "My aunt has written me that you are increasing, India. My felicitations."

"Very coarse expression," Robert remarked before India could respond. Since she thought the same, she swallowed her anger at her mother-in-law's indiscretion and merely bowed her head slightly in acknowledgment of Blanche's remark and went on with her breakfast.

"Don't be so absurdly prudish, Robert. We are all family here, except for Lady Ursula, who doesn't look prudish to me. But then, you were always so, even as a little boy, I remember. So boring, really."

"Well, there you have me, boring and prudish. I am surprised you could bring yourself to propose a visit, under the circumstances," Robert retorted cheerfully.

"I shall not impose myself upon you for longer than it takes me to receive a letter from Lady Benbow, who is always eager for me to come to her."

"Ah, do not say it, Blanche dear, when you have only just arrived," the dowager cried. "Really, Robert, how you can tease her like that!" She rounded upon the advancing footman carrying a plate. "Where are Miss Vernon's eggs? Why must everything in this household take so long? I shall have to speak to Cook about this."

"They are here, my lady," the footman said, setting the plate before Blanche.

"I do pray you to do nothing so foolhardy as to speak to India's cook, Mama." Robert went on before his mother, whose mouth had opened in indignant expostulation, could speak. "I do hope you did not expose yourself to contamination at the Prestons' before coming here, Blanche. I should not care for India to be put in any danger."

"I? Expose myself? You must be all about in your head, Robert, to even think such a thing!"

"Yes, of course, foolish of me," Robert murmured with a grin.

"I saw none of the family at all. I went straight to my room and never left it for the three days while I wrote to Aunt and Lady Benbow. Botts fetched all my meals to me under strict instructions not to go near any of the servants. I was terrified, I can assure you."

"How appreciative your poor hostess must have been of all the trouble you put her to when she had a sick child in the house. I am surprised you stayed at all," Robert said, taking pleasure in goading his cousin into exposing her true nature.

"Where was I to go? The nearest inn was ten miles away and has a reputation for damp sheets and bad food, besides being frightfully dear."

"Naturally you could not go there," the dowager said with a reproachful glance at her son. "You should have got back into the carriage and come on straight to us."

"Another forty miles! I could barely drag myself up the stairs to my room as it was, I was so exhausted. Besides, it was Lord Hartley's carriage, which he had insisted I must have to take me to the Prestons'. I could hardly use it further without his knowledge, though I know he will be most displeased with me when I tell him of it, for he quite dotes on me, the old darling." She smiled smugly.

"How did you get here, then?" Robert asked bluntly. "I feel sure you did not hire a carriage."

She bridled at this. "It was not necessary for me to do so. When I sent Mr. Preston a note inquiring about the hire of one, he wrote back that of course he would send me here in his own carriage. Quite insisted on it, indeed."

Robert was quite sure that Mr. Preston had been only too glad to see the back of such a difficult guest. He contented himself, however, with saying only, "Well, you needn't expect that I will send you on to Lady Benbow's in my carriage, though I will be only too happy to arrange for you to hire one."

"Robert, how rude of you," his mother protested.

"Why, Mama, as Blanche says, we are all family here, including Lady Ursula, whom India and I consider as a sister."

Ursula went quite pink with pleasure and sent him a look of speaking gratitude. However, the hour being somewhat advanced, she rose, saying she must change at once if she was not to keep the Misses Rochdale and Sir Tarquin waiting.

"Is that Tarquin Rochdale?" Blanche asked.

"Yes, my dear," her aunt answered. "He is our neighbor, you know."

"Ah, of course, I think I do just remember him from visits here as a child."

"He has just returned from the West Indies. His family has sugar plantations there."

"Tell the butler to inform me of his arrival and I will go out to speak to him. I recollect meeting him in London some years ago. I am sure he will be happy to meet an old friend."

"I will tell Crigly now. I am going up with Ursula while she changes," India said hastily as she and Ursula left the room.

"Dearest Ursula," India said as they mounted to the next floor, "you must promise not to think badly of Robert for his behavior to Blanche. He really has detested her from childhood. His hackles rise at the mere mention of her name. He can't seem to help himself."

"I would forgive Robert anything except cruelty to you, which thank heaven I shall never see. As for Miss Vernon, she has so barbed a personality she seems to provoke such treatment."

"Yes, she does, which may explain why she has yet to marry. She seems to attract men, but does not succeed in holding them for long, though she wants very much to marry. She is—" India broke off abruptly as a woman carrying a canister of hot water approached them from the back stairs.

"Good morning, my lady," the woman said with a curtsy.

"Good morning, Botts," India replied. "I hope everything is comfortable in Miss Vernon's room?"

"Very comfortable, thank you, my lady."

India walked on then with Ursula, and Botts disappeared

into Blanche's room. "She is Blanche's abigail," India explained as Ursula closed her door behind them, "and reports every word she hears to Blanche. I'll leave you in Carey's hands now and go down to wait for Sir Tarquin, who should be here any moment. But you needn't hurry in the least, since Blanche means to go out to speak to him."

"Does she also know Lord Henry?"

"Oh, heavens, I had forgotten about that. No doubt by now her aunt will have told her all about him. She may very well have met him. She goes about so much that she knows practically everyone."

"Then no doubt she will want to visit him also."

"Not while he is still in his bed, you may be sure of that. Nothing could prevail upon me to allow it."

8

When Ursula came downstairs again she saw through the open front door Blanche in conversation with Sir Tarquin, while the dowager hovered indecisively between them and India, who was talking to the two Misses Rochdale, clearly unwilling to miss anything being said in either conversation.

As Ursula came down the steps to the drive, Blanche lowered her head and then raised her eyes bashfully to Sir Tarquin, as though she had received a compliment, then allowed a ravishing smile to curve her lips. Sir Tarquin looked slightly bewildered by this, but then he saw Ursula and turned to greet her. Before either of them could speak, Blanche continued as though uninterrupted.

" . . . and I must say, Sir Tarquin, that dearly as I would love to join you, I have only arrived not thirty minutes ago and doubt my abigail has had time to unpack my riding dress as yet."

"Oh . . . ah . . . that is too bad. Good morning, Lady Ursula, another lovely day, is it not?"

"Good morning, sir. Indeed it—"

"However," Blanche continued, "if you ride again tomorrow, I shall be happy to join you."

"Our pleasure, Miss Vernon. If you are ready, Lady Ursula?" He led her to her horse and flung her up expertly, while the groom went to assist the young ladies. Ursula waved to India, good-byes were exchanged, and the riding party clattered off down the drive.

"I did hate to disappoint Sir Tarquin when he pressed me to join them," Blanche commented as they turned back to the house. "Come up with me, Aunt, while I wash off this travel dirt and change into another gown."

The two went upstairs and India turned away to hide her grin, for she was as aware as Blanche that far from pressing her to ride, Sir Tarquin had issued no invitation at all, indeed had hardly had a chance to say anything, for Blanche had done all the talking, recalling herself to him and the times they had met in London some years ago.

As they rode away, Ursula said, "So you and Miss Vernon are old friends, Sir Tarquin?"

"I don't know if you could actually call us friends, though I have known her since childhood, or at least that part of it before I went away to school. After that I cannot recall meeting her, though she says we met several times in London before I went to the West Indies. Though I must say I cannot remember it at all."

"Do you miss the West Indies?"

"Good Lord, no! I longed to come home through every moment of my stay there. I knew I could only be happy here, but nothing prepared me for the happiness I have known since I returned. Truly the most exquisite surprise was waiting to repay me for those years away."

"How lovely for you. Am I to know of it?"

"Why, it was finding that you were visiting my nearest neighbor, of course." He smiled very meaningfully into her eyes.

She dropped her own under the warmth of his gaze, but then raised them again and said lightly, "Now, that is as well-polished a compliment as any I've ever heard, Sir Tarquin. I thank you for it."

"I assure you it was meant quite sincerely, Lady Ursula. Indeed, it does not begin to express my feelings. I—"

Before he could continue, Miss Anne Rochdale rode up

beside them to tell them that she wondered at it that Miss Vernon had not acknowledged their introduction to her with even a word, only deigning to nod in their direction.

Ursula was relieved by this interruption, for she was not ready for any discussion of Sir Tarquin's feelings. She hoped very much that such a talk would be postponed indefinitely, even forever, perhaps.

When Ursula returned from her ride, she went up to change at once, and as usual India joined her and they made their way to Lord Henry's room. It had been three days since he had regained consciousness, and every day had seen an improvement, but today they were astonished to find him in a dressing gown sitting in a chair before the fire. His valet, Archer, who had arrived two days before, was hovering solicitously.

"Good morning, ladies. I hope you are surprised," Lord Henry cried, looking very pleased with himself.

"My dear sir, are you sure you should . . . ?" India gasped.

"Very sure, Lady Swanson. I had a lovely steak for breakfast, and the walk from the bed to the chair has given me a fine appetite for my lunch."

"Well, I must say you look very well," India conceded, and indeed he did, for his eyes were clear and shining, and his color restored. It was difficult to equate him with the waxen, unconscious man who had been carried through her door nine days ago.

"Tomorrow I shall dress and come downstairs—I have the doctor's permission," he added hastily to forestall the protest he saw forming on India's lips. "I saw you come back from your ride, Lady Ursula. How I envied you. Poynton sent along one of his horses for me to use when I recover, and I cannot wait until I can join you. Who . . . ah . . . was the gentleman?" he asked casually.

"Sir Tarquin Rochdale, a neighbor of Lady Swanson's,

with his two sisters. They have very kindly asked me to join them in their rides,'' Ursula said.

As she replied, she looked at him and met a very searching look from him, which for some reason caused her to feel a warmth in her cheeks which she prayed he would not notice. He did notice, however, and at once ascribed it to a partiality for Sir Tarquin, and instantly decided that such an unpolished country squire was not good enough for her.

He had thought of her a great deal since he had regained his senses and learned the part she had played in his rescue. Having saved his life, as he thought of it to himself, he felt, unreasonably he knew, that her time should be devoted to him while he was still unwell. He felt quite possessive about her time, and though he would not begrudge her an admirer, surely there would be time for that when he had recovered.

He wished very much to know her better, to know her mind, and to this end he applied himself to regaining his health as quickly as possible in order to get downstairs, for he could never have a private conversation with her while confined to his room, where she must, perforce, always be accompanied by another female.

On the following day, therefore, he watched the departure of the riding party from his window, and then, with Archer's help, had a leisurely bath, dressed, and proceeded to the stairs. Archer tried to support him, but Lord Henry shook him off.

"Don't be such an ass, Archer. Think I'm in my dotage?"

"You are still weak after such an injury, my lord, and you might become dizzy."

"Nonsense. I shall hold the rail, and I don't feel in the least weak." Not for the world would he have admitted, as he proceeded down the stairs, that his legs did tremble slightly and that he was very glad of the banister to hold on to.

"Lord Henry, how wonderful to see you," India said, appearing at the foot of the stairs. "I hope it is not too soon, however."

"Good morning, Lady Swanson. It cannot be too soon for me after lying about for all these days. Surely it is more than enough time to recover from a knock on the head."

He looked handsome, she thought, if rather rakish with the bandage over one side of his forehead, and despite the darkened hollows below his eyes. He gallantly extended his arm for her, which touched her very much. She laid her hand lightly upon it and led him into the drawing room.

She seated him in the corner of a sofa and insisted upon placing a cushion at his back. She ordered wine for him and they settled down for a chat. He questioned her about Lady Ursula's background. She was happy to tell him all about it, including their shared schooldays, their Season together in London, and the subsequent past five years' incarceration with her dying mother. Lord Henry listened raptly and then at the end asked how long had been Lady Ursula's acquaintance with Sir Tarquin, and was much reassured to learn it was only a matter of days. Surely no attachment could have been formed in so short a time.

They were interrupted before he could ask further questions by the entrance of the dowager, who drew up in surprise at the sight of him.

"Mother, may I present Lord Henry Somerton to you. Sir, Robert's mother, Lady Swanson." Lord Henry rose and bowed over her hand.

"Sir, I am of course pleased to make your acquaintance, though I profess myself shocked to find you down so soon after the ordeal you have been through," the dowager said dolefully.

"Oh, I am completely well," he laughed, "and the doctor could not think of any more reasons to keep me in bed."

"Ah, I hope he will not come to regret this undue haste. I only pray it will not cause you to fall into a brain fever."

"Oh, Mother, how very depressing for the poor man on his first day down. I am sure anyone can see Lord Henry is in no danger of such a dire fate."

"I hope you may be right, dear child, but you must remember I have many more years of experience in these matters, and I—"

Before this unprofitable conversation could be continued, the door was opened and Ursula entered, drawing off her gloves, followed by Blanche, resplendent in a bright green riding dress trimmed in black braid and with a little black shako perched impudently upon her blond curls.

"Lord Henry," Ursula cried with a glad smile. "You are down. Crigly told me as we came in, but I had to come make sure for myself before I go up to change." She came forward, holding out her hand. Again he began to rise, but she protested, putting a hand upon his shoulder to prevent him. "No, no, you must stay quite still. I feel sure that was one of the doctor's conditions, and surely we need not stand upon so much ceremony."

He laughed and subsided, then took her proffered hand and kissed it lightly. "Just as you wish, my lady."

"Dear Lord Henry," the dowager gushed, "allow me to present my niece to you, Miss Blanche Vernon."

Blanche came forward and sketched a curtsy, giving him an upward look through her lashes and a shy smile. "Ah, but we are old friends, Lord Henry and I, Aunt."

He looked at her blankly. "I . . . er . . ."

"Oh, dear, how too depressing if you have forgotten, when we stood up for two dances together at Lady Holland's ball last Season."

Lady Holland, one of the great hostesses of London, gave a ball each year, and everyone of consequence was invited, and most would miss it only for a fatal illness or death itself. Not to be there might be interpreted as having not been invited, which heaven forbid!

"I fear you must have mistaken me for someone else, Miss Vernon," Lord Henry said, "for I had to go up to Scotland for my aunt's funeral and did not attend Lady Holland's ball last Season."

Blanche looked staggered for a second, having felt safe in making her untrue statement, since surely he would have been there, and though she had not been invited, she felt he would have forgotten by now with whom he had danced each dance. She made a quick recovery. "Oh, dear, could I have mixed it up with another ball?" She laughed ruefully. "One attends so many, as you know, that after a time they tend to become jumbled in one's mind."

"Just so," he replied with a small sketch of a bow from his seated position, for he could hardly, as a gentleman, persist in denying any previous acquaintance. He turned to Ursula, who had seated herself beside India across from him.

"I hope you enjoyed your ride today."

"Oh, yes, it was heavenly." As she continued to tell him of it, he cursed inwardly at this roomful of women who had frustrated his plan for a private talk with her. He had had no warning of this old woman and her niece being in the house. He came to himself again to find young Lady Swanson addressing him.

" . . . but it has been quite an hour, and I hope you won't think me a nag if I say that in my opinion I think you have had quite enough for your first day downstairs."

"With such company, never," he replied gallantly, though aware suddenly that he felt quite tired and that the thought of his bed was compelling.

"Forgive me if I insist, Lord Henry, but you are a bit pale and I think it best for you to go up now," India said firmly.

He rose at once, and India came quickly to his side. "I will accompany you, if you don't mind, as I must speak to the housekeeper and I believe she is upstairs in the linen room." She took his arm and they left the room.

"Well, I must say he seemed well enough to me," Blanche said poutingly. She had been in a pother since she had heard he was in the house the day before, and persuaded her aunt to accompany her to his room to pay him a visit, so eager was she to meet him. But as they had reached the door,

Robert had come out. Guessing their errand, for he knew Blanche's ways, he had told them that Lord Henry had just dropped off to sleep and could not entertain visitors in any case, and then hurried on downstairs before they could protest. And now, when she at last had met him, he was taken away before she could even properly begin to converse with him.

"Oh, but he did look pale. I am sure India did the right thing in persuading him to retire. It would be dreadful if he had to relapse now that he is at last recovering," Ursula said.

"Tush, nonsense! It is silly to mollycoddle him now he's on his feet again," the dowager said, completely contradicting her earlier dolorous assessment of his case.

"I wonder what ball it was where we had our dances together," Blanche mused. "I was sure it was at the Hollands'."

"Well, I did wonder about it when you said it, dearest girl," the dowager said, "for I remember distinctly how disappointed you were not to have received an invita—"

"Oh, how stupid of me! Of course it was not the Hollands', it was at the Alvanleys' ball in the previous week. How glad I am to have remembered at last. I must tell Lord Henry of my silly mistake. He will be sure to remember."

"Oh, surely he will. But if he does not, it makes no matter, since the poor man has had a dreadful knock on the head and must be still all about in his wits."

Ursula, who found the conversation wearying, rose and said she would go up to change now.

As soon as the door had closed behind her, Blanche turned upon her aunt, her eyes blazing with anger. "Really, if you are going to blurt out my private correspondence to anyone who may be around, I shall have to be more careful in what I confide to you in the future!"

The dowager apologized meekly. Blanche was the only person in the world who could humble her.

9

Blanche appeared for dinner that evening in an elaborate costume of pale lavender crepe embroidered with tiny silver roses, the neck cut low and square, the long sleeves of spider net.

Robert's eyes gleamed with mischief when he saw her. "Heavens, Cousin Blanche, you do us too much honor."

"Yes, she does," the dowager snapped, "but of course she would have presumed you would make up a party to entertain her when she came to visit."

"A party? Dear, dear, how remiss of us. But never mind, we are a family party and must be very jolly. It is too bad Somerton cannot join us."

Blanche, who had been languidly waving a large ostrich-feather fan before her face, stopped abruptly for no more than a half-second, but becoming aware of Robert's eyes upon her, continued, only somewhat less languidly than before. A bright spot of color appeared on each cheek and she cast a brief stony glance at her aunt.

India, sensing that she was upset, interposed quickly. "Oh, but that was never a possibility. Not on his first day out of bed. The doctor would never allow it. Perhaps in a day or so, if he continues to recover well."

The dowager snorted. "I confess I find it ridiculous to suppose that there could be any harm in a man sitting down decently at table to have his meal."

"Not the least in the world," Robert replied agreeably,

"and I make no doubt he is doing so even now. It is the company that makes the difference."

"Do you imply we are not good enough company for the gentleman?" the dowager cried indignantly.

"Oh, nonsense, Mama. Why must you take everything as a personal affront? I meant only that any company when one is ill or recovering from illness makes a social demand that can be tiring."

The atmosphere did not appreciably improve after this. The dowager pouted and spoke only when directly addressed, Blanche looked unutterably bored by whatever was said, and the rest were left to carry on by themselves. They managed cheerfully enough to maintain a conversation, but Ursula felt somewhat damped by the dowager's mien. She did not pay much attention to Blanche beyond politeness, for she felt that she was behaving like a spoilt child who should be ignored for its own good. After all, Blanche had invited herself, and in India's condition it was unfair to expect her to entertain. After dinner the dowager and Blanche excused themselves even before the tea tray was brought in, and retired to their rooms. The climate in the drawing room warmed considerably.

"Do you think Lord Henry will be able to come down for dinner soon, Robert?" India asked as she sat on a stool before her husband, leaning upon his knee.

"Possibly. Up to the doctor, of course."

"I shall ask him in the morning, and when he tells me it will be safe, I shall invite Sir Tarquin to come to dinner," India said.

"Oh, do you think you should be exerting yourself so, dearest?" Ursula protested.

"Pooh! I suppose making the agreeable for a few hours will not hurt me. It is not as though I had to prepare and serve the meal. After all, I suppose it is boring for poor Blanche—"

"Poor Blanche indeed!" Robert snorted. "I warn you, if

you make it too pleasant for her, she will never take herself off. Not with two eligible males to work her wiles on.''

"Oh, Robert, you should not be so hard on Blanche. I feel rather sorry for her," India said chidingly.

"If you had had some of my experiences with her—" Robert began grimly.

"Goodness, Robert, you look very foreboding," Ursula said. "Do tell us what she can have done to make you so unforgiving."

"Many things, but the one I remember most was when she was about ten she found this coachman's whip in the stables and came after me with it. Naturally I ran and she chased me. She tripped and cut her lip open on a rock and ran screaming to the house to report that I had hit her in the mouth with my fist. I got a thundering great beating from my father. He had never beaten me before. I forgave him even while he was doing it, for he cried from the first stroke, but he never forgave himself. Not only for the beating but for not believing me when I denied it, for he knew, really, that I was a truthful child. It preyed on his mind. On his deathbed he asked my forgiveness. That I can't forgive Blanche for. Not the lie, not the tattling, for she was forever doing both those things, but for giving my father pain."

Blanche, in her room, was not thinking of the past. Those lies and the many others she had told over the years were erased from her mind as chalk from a slate. She was hardly aware that she was untruthful. She said whatever assured her comfort, or her getting her own way, and what she said became the truth to her.

The only child of gentle but old-fashioned parents, she had used lies, wiles, and manipulation to get her way from the cradle on. Her parents were unaware of her ruses, not being able to believe so tiny a child could be untruthful, and thus unknowingly spoilt her dreadfully, as well as leaving her barren of any true values.

She was an enchanting little girl with her silvery blond

curls, and was considered the prettiest girl in the county. She went to London prepared to conquer, to be a toast, to receive many proposals, to marry, at last, an earl or even— perhaps—a duke!

None of these things had happened. She was pretty, yes, but not outstandingly so, and her family, while gentlemen and fairly well-off, were neither rich nor distinguished enough to give her cachet. She had a dowry of six thousand pounds, which was not to be sneezed at, but was not enough to draw the more desirable *partis*. She received two proposals in her first Season, one from the third son of a viscount, an impecunious young man with no expectations whatever and an enormous appetite for gambling. The other offer was from a young squire's son.

Neither of these offers would she even deign to consider, and she retired to the country to lick her wounds and plan her campaign for the next Season. Season after Season had followed, however, with no better luck. She was totally unaware that though she could attract men who would dance with her, call upon her, send her posies, and take her riding in the park, her desperate need to be married would at last become apparent through the surface charm and frighten the gentlemen away after a week or so. At least it did so to the ones she would consider. The ones she would not were in need of her dowry or too green and fresh from the country to recognize anything but her blond good looks and her air of fashion.

Now she found herself in the most promising position she had been in for many years. A guest in the house that contained Lord Henry Somerton, and a neighbor who called daily, Sir Tarquin Rochdale, both highly eligible and acceptable.

She had, before she had learned anything of Lord Henry, decided that she could very easily have Sir Tarquin if she chose. True, he was seemingly calling to see Lady Ursula, but Blanche felt this was not competition to even be considered. If she could not turn him from any feelings he may have developed toward Lady Ursula, she, Blanche, was not the girl she thought herself!

Now, however, having met Lord Henry, there was no question in her mind of which she would have. No "catch" could be greater than Lord Henry Somerton. Bringing him up to scratch had been the aim of every London mama with a marriageable daughter for at least five years. And now, here he was, to be seen every day, still vulnerable from his accident and needing a soft shoulder to lean upon and sympathetic eyes to smile into his.

Sir Tarquin's presence, moreover, was all to the good. Though she now felt he was beneath her touch for marriage, his encouragement to develop a *tendre* for her would help, no doubt, to rouse Lord Henry to compete. Everyone knew that men always felt such situations as a challenge, always flocked to the honeypot already attracting bees.

She made her plans and, accordingly, sent down word the next morning that she was feeling tired and would have breakfast in her room and a quiet day. Though her room did not face the front of the house, as did Lord Henry's, she could hear quite clearly the clatter of the riding party assembling and, later, clopping off down the drive. Then she rose and set about arraying herself for the morning.

Just as her abigail was lowering a peach-blossom muslin over her head, a tap at the door heralded the entrance of the dowager. "My dear child, you are up? I made sure you were ill when you did not come down to breakfast and said you would not ride."

"Why should you think that? I did not say I was ill. Only that I wanted a quiet day," Blanche reported ungraciously.

"I am glad to hear I was wrong. Will you like me to walk in the shrubberies with you?"

"No, thank you. I shall just go down quietly to the drawing room."

"Very well, my dear. I will fetch my work basket and join you."

"Please do not think of it. I believe I shall find Lord Henry there for company, and I shall not welcome a chaperone," she added, knowing what her aunt's next words would be.

"But, Blanche, my child, surely . . . Oh, well . . . Of course, if you . . ." The dowager's shock subsided under Blanche's steely look.

Sometime later, when Blanche heard a firm tread in the corridor, she peeked out her door in time to see Lord Henry descending the stairs. She quietly closed the door and returned to her dressing table. There she checked her hair and the set of her gown, and after a moment's contemplation of her face, took up her rouge pot and added a touch of color to her cheeks and lips. She smiled at herself in satisfaction.

Lord Henry had, that morning, been visited by Robert, who brought with him the London papers and an invitation to use his library if he liked, rather than the drawing room. Shortly after this the doctor came in, pronounced himself not too displeased with his patient's condition, and gave him permission to go downstairs again during the morning.

Petitioned by India as he was leaving, the doctor agreed that if nothing occurred today to overtire his patient then he might be fit enough to take his dinner in company in the evening.

Lord Henry also heard the riding party assembling and then trotting off. He did not look out his window, for he did not care to see Sir Tarquin strutting about and throwing Lady Ursula into the saddle in a way Lord Henry condemned as vulgar showing off. He dressed, and with Robert's newspapers, descended to the library, where he looked forward to a quiet morning reading all the latest news and gossip while he awaited the return of the riding party.

Blanche was halfway down the stairs when she halted and drew back as India came out of the drawing room and then moved out of sight toward the back of the house. Blanche continued down and entered the drawing room, prepared to give a start of surprise at finding Lord Henry there. She stared about in disbelief. He was not there! Where could he be? She checked the two other reception rooms that opened out of the drawing room but were kept closed off unless there was a party, but found no sight of her quarry. Across the hall was the ballroom, the same size as the three drawing rooms, but she discounted any idea of finding him there. Below, on the first floor, were the dining room, the break-fast room, the kitchens, and—ah, yes—Robert's library!

She went down, and throwing open the library door, was able to give quite a creditable start of surprise at finding Lord Henry there. She widened her eyes and covered her "Oh" of surprise with her hand. "Oh, I did not realize . . . Please forgive my . . . I . . . I . . ."

Lord Henry threw down the papers he was reading and rose. "I'm sorry to have startled you, Miss . . . er . . . Vernon," he said with a bow.

"Oh, no, you must not apologize. It is for me to do so for disturbing you. I am having a quiet day and came for a book. Cousin Robert always begs me to help myself. I won't intrude for more than a moment." She hurried to a bookcase and took down a book and turned to go.

"Won't you sit down for just a moment, Miss Vernon?" Lord Henry asked, not averse to the company of a pretty girl. Well, not a girl, he thought after a second look.

"But I would not disturb you for the world!"

"Not in the least. I was only reading the latest *on-dits*. Have you met this Mrs. H-F they speak of so guardedly?"

"Oh, no, sir, I have not met her. We hardly move in the same circles. She is a Mrs. Hellmont-Ferbin, a widow, as I have heard, who has not entrée to respectable drawing rooms."

"Ah, I see. One of Prinny's . . . er . . . friends, is she?"

"Well, I have heard that the Prince Regent has taken a somewhat particular interest," Blanche said, casting down her eyes and wishing desperately that she could call up a blush.

They continued their conversation along these lines for some ten minutes or so before the door opened to admit India.

"Lord Henry, I have ordered you some—" India halted in astonishment at the sight of Blanche. "Good heavens, Blanche, I thought you had the headache and would be upon your bed. I was just going to come up to you after I had offered Lord Henry some wine and biscuits."

"I cannot see why everyone must assume I am ill just because I did not feel like riding today," Blanche said crossly. Then, realizing Lord Henry was looking at her with a raised brow, she added, "But, dearest India, how very kind of you to think of me. Is she not the kindest person in the world, Lord Henry?" She cast an appealing smile at him.

In an instant India saw Blanche's entire plan and replied blandly, "Well, I am sure I am glad to learn that you are well after all, Blanche. Perhaps you would like some wine also?" She crossed to pull the bell rope, and when Crigly entered, ordered the refreshments. She then came to seat herself upon the sofa beside Blanche, and turned upon her a blinding smile. "Well, now, isn't this lovely. Though we may not ride, we can have a nice quiet conversation all together and entertain ourselves. I do so love to have company."

10

"You will not credit it, dearest, but there she was all cozy in Robert's library with Lord Henry for goodness knows how long," India said indignantly.

She had come up to Ursula's room with her when the riding party had returned. Ursula had been helped out of her habit by Carey and into a primrose lawn morning dress. When Carey had gone away, India had described the scene she had come upon earlier.

"But why ever should she not be?" Ursula protested with a laugh.

"Because . . . well . . . I don't know exactly, but it's deceitful! Pretending not to feel well enough to ride, and . . . and . . ."

"Perhaps she did not."

"Nonsense. You are too softhearted. I am too well up on Blanche's ways not to recognize it was a well-thought-out plan to be alone with him. I am sure she forbade my mother-in-law to come down with her, or she would have been there. She dotes on Blanche and follows her about like a faithful dog when she is here."

"Come, India, what can it matter if she chose to spend the morning alone with him?"

"He is still vulnerable after his injury, and she might . . . might . . ."

"Trap him into a declaration? Now you are being a goose. I doubt any woman could trap him into anything he had no mind for after all his years of experience with the determined mamas of London.''

''But he is still weak!''

''In the knees perhaps, not in his senses. He has not lost his wits for all he got a knock on the head. Have no fear on that score. He is well able to defend himself, and if he could bring himself to care for such a woman as Blanche, then he . . .''

''Yes . . . what?''

''Then they will both get what they deserve,'' Ursula declared, feeling a blush warming her cheeks.

''There, I knew you did not like her.''

''No, I do not. I find her rude and spoilt and cold, but that does not mean I wish her harm. You said before to Robert that you felt sorry for her, and that has made me think. You are right. There is something pitiable about her. I suppose she must be quite desperate to marry. It is a dreadful burden upon a woman, to feel she has no worth as a human being until some man confers the blessing of his name upon her.''

''Oh, darling, of course it is too horrible for her. I do wonder why she has not taken. She was a pretty girl, you know, from a good family and creditable dowry. Robert says that she has had offers, but refused them all. He says she was holding out for a title. And now of course she is so old—''

''Surely not more than two or three years older than I. However, I am glad to say I have no thought to marry. I like my independence too much, now that I have finally attained it, to want to give it up for any man.''

India laughed. ''Oh, you will feel quite differently when you meet someone right for you.''

''Perhaps. I don't say I have closed my mind on the subject. I hope I would not be so silly. But I shan't be on the lookout or setting traps or anything of that sort.''

''You could not, nor will you have to. You are . . .

oh . . ." India paused, and a look of wonder came into her eyes.

"What? What is it, dearest? Are you ill?"

"No . . . it . . . it moved!" She put her hand gently against her stomach. "Oh, Ursula, it moved!"

After this momentous event, all thoughts of Blanche and marriage went out the window and they settled down happily to talk of motherhood.

At dinner that evening Blanche, having made sure Lord Henry would be coming down for it by asking that gentleman himself, appeared again in her extravagantly lovely lavender gown. Ursula wore one of the three lesser evening gowns she had brought with her for family occasions. Blanche eyed it superciliously, then looked down at her own gown complacently.

Good heavens, Ursula thought, one can practically see her thoughts written upon her face. She looked up quickly, hoping for some reason that Blanche's thoughts had not been read by anyone else, particularly Robert, who might say something cutting to her if he suspected her of looking down upon his wife's best friend. The eyes she caught, however, were Lord Henry's, and it seemed to her there was a glimmer of amusement there, and complicity in some shared thoughts, in the look he gave her.

He bent attentively, however, to Blanche when she began to speak to him in a low voice, as though to exclude the rest of the party from their intimate conversation. He managed adroitly to include everyone at the table in his responses, until, puzzled and frustrated, she desisted.

The ladies withdrew and left the men to their port, but they did not linger over it for long. In the drawing room Blanche had seated herself upon a small sofa and spread her skirts over it. When the men came in, she looked up eagerly at Lord Henry and moved her skirts aside in a clear invitation.

He seemed not to see this, however, and walked past her to where Ursula sat beside India on a sofa near the open

French doors. The night was still and warm, and the scent from the garden drifted in, a mixture of roses, night stock, and tobacco flowers.

"My dear Lady Swanson, I must congratulate you upon your cook. That was a most delicious dinner, and it's grand to be in company once again."

"Thank you, sir. We were very happy to have you at table with us at last. I only hope you will take no harm from so much company thrown upon you all at once. Are you tired?"

"Good Lord, no. I only suffer from a need to walk off my overindulgence at your excellent table. I was wondering if I could tempt you ladies to take a turn on the terrace with me."

India rose briskly. "What a delightful idea. Come along, Ursula. We shan't even need shawls, I think, it is so warm."

The three exited through the French doors under the infuriated eyes of Blanche. The dowager looked agitated. "Oh, dear, Robert, you surely must insist that dear India come in at once. The night air is so dangerous, and she hasn't even a shawl. Her condition, you know." She added this last in a conspiratorial whisper.

"Her condition," Robert said loudly, "is incipient motherhood, not a wasting disease."

"But, Robert, you must . . . Oh, it is too bad of you to treat with such levity so serious a matter. You grow more and more like your dear father. He used to do the same thing. I do implore you to—"

"Oh, very well, Mama, don't fuss." As the trio passed the open doors, he called out, "India, I insist that you come in from that dangerous night air at once—and come and entertain your husband."

India looked around, grinned, and disengaging her hand from Lord Henry's arm, skipped inside to throw herself at her husband's feet. "At your will, my lord," she said in her humblest tones.

He laughed and tumbled her bright auburn curls. "Minx," he whispered lovingly.

Lord Henry and Ursula watched this scene and then passed again out of sight.

"How fortunate they are," Lord Henry said.

"And deserving of it," Ursula said, "they are so very good."

"Alas, the deserving are not always so fortunate. I myself, for example, can claim to be deserving, but such fortune as is theirs has eluded me."

"Oh, dear. I fear your injury has turned your thoughts too much inward, sir, and caused you to fall into a melancholia," she chided with a smile.

"Not a bit of it," he assserted. "I am not in the least melancholic, I assure you. I speak but the truth. I am an upstanding, God-fearing Englishman, a fair and benevolent landlord, kind to animals, firm but understanding with my servants, and a doting uncle to my sister's children, who fortunately live in the Scottish Highlands and rarely make demands upon me."

She laughed aloud at this, and he looked down upon her in a gratified way. "There, now, I have amused you, thank heaven."

"Why should you thank heaven for that?" she asked, tilting her head to look up at him, still laughing.

"I have a heavy debt, Lady Ursula, and must pay it as best I can."

"Now, if we are going to go on in that vein, I shall not listen to you anymore," she said hastily, attempting to pull her hand from his arm.

He quickly put his own over hers to retain it. "I surrender. No more in that vein, I promise. Shall we talk instead of what I was thinking before I received that crack on the head?"

"Of what you were thinking?"

"Yes. You see, the evening before, at an inn, I briefly glimpsed the most remarkable pair of blue eyes—"

"Oh!" she exclaimed with a startled look at him.

"Yes. Beautiful blue eyes that seemed to follow me down into the darkness when I fell, for from time to time I thought they were looking at me so compellingly. Then—think of it—the darkness finally lifted and I opened my eyes and there they were, very near, looking straight into my own, and a soft little hand was holding mine. It remains as my happiest memory—to date," he added with a smile and a meaningful look, holding her eyes captive. After what seemed aeons she managed to drag her own away from his and felt a slow blush mounting her cheeks.

"I . . . You . . . you refine too much upon . . . After all, you had had such a dreadful fall, and . . . and . . ."

"And was delirious? No, no, my dear, that will not answer. You see, as I rode away from the inn that morning, it was with the utmost depression. The stableboy, devil take him, told me that you were a Lady Liddiard, and so I assumed you were married. If he had said Lady Ursula Liddiard, nothing could have persuaded me to leave without seeing you again. As it was, it was as though fate had shown me where happiness lay and then laughed at my presumption in wanting it. If I had not been so blue-deviled, I would never have been thrown from my horse at all."

His words had set her pulses pounding and her head was spinning. Could he really be saying . . . ? But no, he could not be. She wished she could be quite alone for a time to go over it all in her mind and try to understand. At last she managed a somewhat shaky laugh. "Oh, I see it all now. Your pride has been as much damaged as your head, and you are casting about for someone to blame your fall upon."

He stared at her for a second and then gave a great shout of laughter. "Oh, you little minx! A very neat shot across the bows, but it shall not serve, for I intend—"

At that moment they heard Crigly announcing to the drawing room, "Sir Tarquin Rochdale, my lord."

"Blast!" Henry said feelingly. "Come away down the terrace quickly. We'll pretend we did not hear."

"Why, we cannot do anything so rude. We must go in at once," Ursula protested, rather glad than otherwise to have this interruption, for she was not sure she could think coherently if he continued in this strain any longer. She needed to think about it: was he teasing her, or was it only another way of "paying a debt"? She hurried into the drawing room.

Sir Tarquin was saying, "I do hope you will not mind this intrusion at so late an hour, Lady Swanson. I am just on my way home from dinner with the Peckhams and thought I would stop in for just a moment to inquire about Miss Vernon's health."

"Not at all, my dear sir. You are most welcome, indeed. As for Miss Vernon, she must answer for herself," India said.

Sir Tarquin trod across the floor to bend over the dowager's hand, then India's, before turning to Blanche. She had been moping sullenly an instant before, but now sat up, eyes sparkling, smiling prettily. "How very kind, Sir Tarquin," she said, holding out her hand. "I assure you it was only an inclination to be lazy that kept me from riding today, not an indisposition."

"I am most gratified to hear it."

Then he became aware of Ursula entering from the terrace with Lord Henry behind her and went forward to greet her and be introduced. The two gentlemen bowed stiffly to one another.

When Sir Tarquin turned back, Blanche smiled at him and pulled aside her skirts in invitation and he went to sit beside her. Ursula sat across from them on a sofa beside India, and Lord Henry subsided into a chair beside Ursula. The conversation became general for a time, though Blanche monopolized it as much as she could, casting flirtatious sallies at Sir Tarquin and sparkling eyes upon Lord Henry. She noticed he seemed to be eyeing Sir Tarquin in a less-than-friendly way and immediately decided he was becoming jealous of Sir Tarquin for finding favor in her eyes. She became even more vivacious, forcing Sir Tarquin's attention back to herself each time he turned to speak to anyone else.

Ursula and India exchanged carefully blank glances, and neither dared look at Robert, whose cynical eyebrow had nearly reached his hairline as he watched Blanche's performance, his lips twitching.

The dowager aided her niece to the best of her ability by laughing extravagantly at everything she said and exclaiming upon her wit.

At last, after a quarter of an hour the tea tray was brought in, and after drinking a cup, Sir Tarquin rose. "Now, I must not presume upon your good nature another moment. It is quite late and I must be on my way."

"You know well how welcome you are in this house at any time, Sir Tarquin. Indeed, I hope we can persuade you upon very short notice to dine with us tomorrow, if you are not already engaged," India said.

"How kind. I would be most delighted," he said, and then went around to bid each lady good night. Robert accompanied him out to the hall.

"I shall send a note to Mr. Phillips-Glenn-Phillips first thing in the morning and invite him to make up the table," India said.

"Good heavens, that old court card," the dowager cried. "He will not amuse Blanche in the least. Surely there is a younger man you could ask?"

"Blanche has two young men to amuse her already," Robert said dryly as he reentered the room. "Another might try even her resources."

"Nonsense," his mother said.

"Besides, I like Mr. Phillips-Glenn-Phillips, and I must also be amused," Robert said.

The dowager subsided. Later, when she went up to bed with Blanche, she received a scolding. "How could you be so stupid as not to see that forcing India to come in left Lord Henry and Ursula alone out there together?" Blanche said crossly. However, her heart was not really in it. She was too filled with her triumph at the end of the evening to bother. Besides, Ursula was not the type to become in the least flirtatious with a man when opportunity arose, and much good would it have done her if she had, she was such a poor dowdy little thing. Not at all Lord Henry's type. She remembered that Chaist girl, and several others, all tall and blond, just as she was. She was his type!

11

Blanche rode the next morning, for not to do so might cast some doubt on her motive of yesterday, and might cause Lord Henry to think she was pursuing him. After her success of the evening before, she must let his jealousy grow by seeing her ride out with Sir Tarquin.

She was still irritated with her aunt for being so stupid the evening before, but there was nothing to be done about it now, and no doubt it meant very little in any case. Naturally, Sir Henry was grateful to the girl for her help on the road and would want to show her every courtesy, but he could never develop a partiality for such a dab of a creature. Why, she already behaved like a spinster, with no attempt at witty conversation, never using her eyes, her only good feature, really, never flirting. Gentlemen liked to be flirted with. It made them feel no end of a devil and boosted their ego. Any schoolgirl could tell you so, but Lady Ursula seemed to be totally innocent in such matters.

Indeed, Blanche was right in this, for Ursula was not only unschooled in the art; she thought that it was a vulgar accomplishment. She had been very well aware that Lord Henry had been about to pay her another compliment when they were on the terrace, but the knowledge had set up such a turmoil of conflicting emotions at the time that she had seen Sir Tarquin's entrance as a blessed reprieve. She was not so unnatural that she despised compliments, but for some reason she did not want to hear one from him, did not want to let herself experience the pleasure it might give her, lest it unleash emotions in herself that she knew would cause unhappiness for her in the end. Lord Henry, as she knew, was very well schooled in the art of flirtation, and what would be for him a light moment, soon forgotten, which he would expect her to respond to in kind, might be dangerous for her own peace of mind.

Not that she thought all this out explicitly in her mind, but she seemed to know it instinctively and act upon it blindly. If she had thought about it, she might have wondered why she found Sir Tarquin's compliments unthreatening, his flirtation only amusing, his presence at tonight's dinner something she could look forward to without a moment's flutter.

They all rode out together, with India and Lord Henry waving to them from the steps. Sir Tarquin divided his attentions equally between the two ladies. There was some juggling on Blanche's part to ride next to him when the path narrowed, but when Ursula saw this, she fell back cheerfully to the company of Miss Rochdale and Miss Anne. Miss Vernon, she thought, certainly showed a lack of subtlety in her maneuverings.

Ursula dressed for dinner in one of her gowns saved for an occasion when India would have guests for dinner. It was a blue-violet gauze over blue satin, with a simple strand of pearls given to her by her godmother at her come-out and her mother's sapphire earrings. She felt she looked quite grand until she saw Blanche. She smiled ruefully to herself at her own naiveté.

Blanche delayed her entrance until all the guests had assembled. She wore an elaborate gown of lemon sarcenet trimmed at the bottom with embroidered roses under white lace, and fastened down the front with topaz clasps. She wore a topaz necklace and earrings and a richly embroidered lemon gauze scarf draped carelessly over her elbows.

She looked very grand indeed, much too grand for a small dinner party in the country. India and Ursula exchanged one of their blank-faced looks, perfected during their school years together, that spoke volumes to one another, but expressed nothing to any onlooker, and then both looked quickly away. As Ursula's eyes turned away, she thought she caught a trace of a minutely raised brow and a twitch at the corner of Lord Henry's lips, but she could not be sure. She looked away immediately, not wanting to catch his eye.

Robert rose to the occasion. "Again you astonish us, Cousin," he said, grinning. "You make me feel uneasily that I might not have removed all the straw from my hair."

Blanche's eyes flashed, but she smothered her angry retort and tapped him playfully on the cheek with her fan. "I doubt you are uneasy in the least, Robert, since you so enjoy portraying yourself as a country bumpkin."

"Ah, children, children, you mustn't tease one another. But it was ever so, even as children," the dowager said indulgently.

"Allow me to present you to Mr. Phillips-Glenn-Phillips, Cousin. Sir, Miss Blanche Vernon."

Mr. Phillips-Glenn-Phillips tripped forward, bowed profoundly, and kissed the hand Blanche extended to him. His white hair was long and pulled back and tied with a black ribbon to resemble the wig he had worn as a young man. His clothing also spoke of the previous century, being fawn satin knee breeches, white stockings and black pumps, and a blue satin dress coat with gilt buttons over a white marcella waistcoat. He was an agreeable-looking old gentleman with rosy cheeks and merry blue eyes.

He retained Blanche's hand and smiled appreciatively at her glittering blond beauty. "Well, well, my dear, what a delightful surprise to find not only our lovely hostess, but two other beautiful young ladies at the same dinner table. And this," he added with aplomb, "apart from the pleasure of seeing my old friend Lady Swanson again." He turned to bow to the dowager.

Blanche smiled politely and turned away without replying.

She had no interest in, or time to waste on, the old gentleman, or indeed on any old gentleman unless she should have the good fortune to meet an elderly, unmarried duke with no children, still interested in begetting an heir. A very wealthy old duke, needless to say, to make it worth her while. But such a person had never come her way, nor was likely to.

"Well, perhaps we could go in to dinner now that you have at last graced us with your presence, Cousin," Robert said. "I expect that you have forgotten that we country bumpkins eat our mutton early."

"What a vulgar expression, my son," the dowager reproved.

"Country bumpkin? But you did not take exception to Blanche's using it," Robert said.

"Come, Robert," India said hastily, "do you take Ursula in to dinner. Lord Henry, if you would take our mother, and Sir Tarquin Miss Vernon. I shall claim Mr. Phillips-Glenn-Phillips' arm."

Robert and India sat at either end of the table, with Ursula on Robert's right, Lord Henry beside her, and the dowager on his right. On India's right sat Sir Tarquin, with Blanche between him and Mr. Phillips-Glenn-Phillips. Not the ideal arrangement, but with only four couples it was not easy to better it, taking into account other difficulties, such as not seating Blanche near Robert and making sure the dowager had no cause to complain about being slighted.

Blanche looked displeased with her position, but at least she had Sir Tarquin beside her and Lord Henry facing her. She made the most of it by sending sparkling smiles across the table at him at every opportunity, and tossing quips to him from time to time, meantime demanding nearly full-time attention from Sir Tarquin, calling him to heel each time he attempted to pass a few words with India. Mr. Phillips-Glenn-Phillips she ignored.

Lord Henry missed most of Blanche's smiles and was unable to respond to her quips, since the dowager had him by the ear, taking him through a very exacting genealogical examination by which she was able to prove, to her own triumphant satisfaction, that a son from a minor branch of his family had some eighty years previously married the daughter of a Youngreaves connection, and this was conclusive evidence that they were related. Lord Henry looked a trifle bemused, but agreed good-naturedly that it must be so.

India felt a bit put out at having no one at all to speak with. She saw that Ursula was in much the same situation, for though Robert and Mr. Phillips-Glenn-Phillips tried to include her in their conversation, they were discussing county families whom she did not know; she could therefore make no contribution to the conversation, much less find it interesting.

India stared at her compellingly until at last Ursula looked up, and then India blinked her eyes very slowly, an agreed signal between them that meant "Follow me." This could be intended literally or interpreted as "Do as I do." Since they could hardly leave the table, in this case it must mean the latter.

When Blanche paused for a moment to take a bite of her chicken à la tarragon, India turned full upon Sir Tarquin and began talking to him with great animation and even greater determination. When Blanche turned to him again, she was met by his shoulder, and though she tried very hard to regain his attention, it was impossible, without great rudeness to her hostess.

Ursula knew she was supposed now to usurp Lord Henry from the dowager, and though she feared her ability was not equal to India's, and dreaded the dowager's reaction, she turned to Lord Henry resolutely. Since the dowager was now attending to her plate with gusto, it was not so difficult as it might have been.

"I think your friend Mr. Poynton must be very sorry to have missed your visit," she said, striking out blindly with the first thing that came to her mind. She felt a fool for such an inane opening, but Lord Henry, turning to her gratefully, did not seem to mind.

"Oh, yes, he sent a note by my man with his regrets. But I see him every summer for the fishing, so we shall make it up later. He has a nice bit of water on his property, with grand fishing. And then usually I go for some shooting in September as well, so we see enough of one another."

"I suppose you see him in London during the Season also?"

"Not he! He despises London. Never leaves Sussex unless he's forced to go up to the dentist or on business. Do you like London?"

"I liked the little time I spent there. But of course, it was when I was young—for my come-out—so it was all parties and balls, and very exciting. I have never been since."

"When you were young," he said teasingly. "And now, being of such great age, you would not enjoy it, I suppose."

"Oh, yes, I think I might, but for different reasons. I should like to see all the sights: the Tower, the Wax Museum, Vauxhall Gardens."

"What, no balls, no *fêtes champêtres*?"

"I doubt I would know anyone any longer to invite me after five years away."

"Is that when you made your come-out? Five years ago? Why, I was in London then."

"Yes, I know. I saw you at several balls."

"And we did not meet?"

"Oh, yes, we were introduced once."

"Impossible! I could not have come face-to-face with those eyes and forgotten it!"

"Well," she replied with a twinkle, "you were much taken with a Miss Chaist, as I remember it."

"Good God! Marianne Chaist! So I was. And I doubt I've thought of her more than once since. Yes, it was only once— when I read in the paper that she had snared a marquess. I was quite surprised, because she had always made it very clear that she was interested only in the eldest son of a duke. A younger son would not do her at all, so I was very soon given my marching orders.''

Since he was grinning reminiscently and there was not the least trace of residual regret in his tone, she concluded he had not been so smitten with the beautiful Miss Chaist as she had thought at the time. Her spirits rose inexplicably.

"Poor Miss Chaist," she said.

"Why? Because she did not become a duchess after all?"

"Oh, no, because she should have set her heart on being one in the first place. It is so vain and heartless, I think. Where are love and respect for one's future mate in such a program?"

"Oh, I don't believe those requirements came very high on her list," he said with a laugh.

"But what if after marrying she found he was a profligate, a wastrel, or of a cruel nature?"

"She would still be a duchess," he said wryly.

"How very dreadful. To take such a dangerous chance—one that involves the rest of her life—only to have a title. How could it mean so much to her, when she might not love him, or perhaps with the possibility of never being able to learn to love him, for I am not so stupid as to think that all marriages are love matches, but surely if one starts out with respect for the other, and if they are both of good nature and kindliness, they come to be very happy together after all. Oh, dear, I beg your pardon for sermonizing," she said with a blush.

"Not the least. I like to hear sincere feeling expressed. I agree with your sentiments entirely. One of the things that put me off London was that mercenary pursuit of husbands or heiresses."

"Well, I have had no experience of that, not being an heiress, though I make no doubt you were much beset," she added teasingly.

He laughed but made no reply, modesty forbidding him

to agree, and honesty precluding a disclaimer. The table now
having been cleared, India rose to lead the ladies back to
the drawing room, warning the men not to linger too long
over their wine. Blanche flounced upstairs to repair any
disarrangement of hair or dress, and the dowager looked after
her nervously, knowing her niece was out of temper, and
at last hurried upstairs after her.

"Well, dearest, I could see you were having no difficulty
with Lord Henry," India said when they were alone.

"Nor you with Sir Tarquin," Ursula returned, "but I fear
we were rude to behave so."

"Nonsense! We did no more than what was being done
to us through the first two courses. Really, Blanche is a
menace, trying to dominate every eligible man at once. That
is rudeness, if you like, because it is so selfish."

"Come, let us play some duets. I used to think so longingly
of our duets when I had to remain at home. They were such
fun."

They sat down at the pianoforte and went through the music
until they found pieces they had used to play together, and
then, with much urging to hurry or pleas to go slower, and
a great deal of giggling, they worked through several pieces.

Blanche and her aunt returned. Blanche took up a book,
but tossed it aside when she discovered it was a book of
sermons. She then sat staring broodingly into the fire until
the gentlemen came in. Ursula and India rose hastily, but
the men begged them to go on.

"Oh, dear me, we could not," Ursula protested. "We have
only been amusing ourselves. We must practice together for
a time before we will be ready to perform in the drawing
room."

India suggested that Blanche might play for them, but she
refused. Being an indifferent performer, she felt she did not
shine at the pianoforte.

Lord Henry said, "May I suggest that we all have a stroll

on the terrace? It is just such another wonderful night as last night.''

"Oh, lovely,'' Blanche cried, jumping up at once, hand outstretched to take his arm. Lord Henry, however, was already holding out his arm to Ursula and did not see her. Blanche turned to Sir Tarquin, who obligingly held out his arm, while Robert put his arm about his wife's waist and led the way out onto the terrace.

The dowager declined to move, and Mr. Phillips-Glenn-Phillips gallantly declared he was very glad of this, as he had had no opportunity to speak with her at all.

The young people strolled up and down the terrace in the soft darkness, with the moon just rising over the trees and a nightingale calling enchantingly from the woods. All Blanche's attempts to merge the couples were foiled by Henry and Robert. Robert ignored her and Henry turned Ursula about and walked firmly away to the other end of the terrace.

"I do so want to go on with our conversation at dinner, Lady Ursula,'' he said, drawing her hand through his arm.

"Our conversation?''

"Yes. The one about marriage. You have some very interesting ideas for one so young. Where have you acquired them?''

"Well, obviously not through experience,'' she quipped. "In fact, my only knowledge of marriage is based completely upon observation. First, of my parents, where I learned what bitterness can grow between two mismatched people who marry for the wrong reasons.''

"What were their reasons?''

"My father needed money. My mother wanted a title. They both got what they wanted, so they should have been happy, but they were not. Then there are my brother and his Albinia.''

"From your tone, I take it you do not care for Albinia.''

"I do not dislike her unless I have too much of her

company. She has aspirations to be an invalid and, being healthy as a horse, has had to fall back upon her nerves to support her ambitions. Since Rupert likes to fuss over people, I suppose you could call it a happy marriage, but sometimes I think I see a desperate gleam in his eye when she calls him to her side once again. Perhaps I only imagine it. In any case, such a marriage would not appeal to me.''

''What does appeal to you?''

''Robert and India.''

''Of course. We are at one in that, for you must recall last night when we walked after dinner, I told you how deserving I am of just such happiness as theirs in marriage. And I believe, long though it has been kept out of my reach, I am now very near to achieving it.''

''I wish you every success, Lord Henry, for I'm sure you do deserve it,'' she said quite sincerely.

He bent his head nearer to hers and said softly, ''If you really mean that, then I am more confident than ever of my success.''

Ursula became completely confused and hurriedly steered the conversation away from marriage. He saw what she was doing and allowed her to have her way, for he felt very confident of her now. She was as shy and nervous as a young fawn, but he felt he had all the time in the world to teach her to love. He had no doubts of eventually winning her, for he could not afford doubts. He must win her!

12

Lord Henry, to everyone's surprise, came down for breakfast the next morning, looking very rested despite his exertions at the dinner party the evening before. The doctor had not yet come to give his permission for this morning expedition, but Lord Henry felt well enough now to make his own decisions.

Naturally, the dowager could not suppress her doubts about the wisdom of his decision. "My dear sir, I think you are most rash not to have stayed in your bed all morning to recover from yesterday's dissipations. Most unwise, in my opinion."

"My dear Lady Swanson, I will be open with you. I do so detest eating from a tray in bed that had I been so weak as to have been unable to walk downstairs, I should have had myself carried down. As it is, I think I have never felt better or more filled with energy—a result of all that enforced rest, I suppose." He bowed to her and turned to India. "Good morning, dear Lady Swanson, Lady Ursula, Miss Vernon. Good morning, Robert."

They all greeted him and he took an empty chair next to Ursula and ordered a beefsteak, eggs, and toast, and accepted a plate of ham from Crigly to stay him in the meantime.

"Do you ride today, Lady Ursula?" he asked as he cut into his ham.

"If the weather holds. It is something overcast, however."

"Ah, if only I could join you. I long for exercise. I shall

105

ask the doctor today how soon I may be allowed to ride.''

"Good heavens, Lord Henry," Blanche cried, "how can you be so brave after so disastrous a fall?''

"Oh, I know it looked bad, but certainly not the worst fall I've had by any means. Over the years I've broken one arm, one leg, and my collarbone. Any one of those was more painful, took longer to heal, and was more irritating than a knock on the head.''

"But how dreadful! Now, I have never fallen from my horse," Blanche declared proudly.

"That must be because of your superior horsemanship, Blanche. I wish I could claim the same, for I have had many bad falls," Robert said ironically.

"Oh, dear boy, do you remember the time we were sure you had broken your back and it turned out to be only a very bad bruising? You could not move for a week," his mother cried.

"And I once broke my wrist, apart from several falls that bruised my pride more than anything else," Ursula confessed.

"Lord, you make me feel left out for having no injuries to recount," Blanche said gaily, though still smarting from Robert's remark.

"Never mind, dear child," the dowager soothed. "I myself have never fallen from a horse.''

"How could you, Mama, when you have never ridden a horse?" Robert said.

This caused a general burst of hilarity, in the midst of which the door flew open to admit a round little lady with Crigly hovering anxiously behind her.

"Henry!" the lady cried, and without another word sank backward into Crigly's arms in a dead faint.

"My God!" Henry exclaimed, thrusting back his chair and rushing around the table. Everyone rose and followed him in alarm.

"Who is it, Lord Henry?" India asked, falling to her knees

beside the body, which Crigly, unequal to the sudden dead-weight, had staggered backward with a few steps before gently easing her to the floor. Without waiting for an answer, India called for hartshorn and water and loosened the lady's bonnet strings. The dowager produced a vinaigrette from her reticule, which India accepted and waved before the lady's nose.

"I . . . I cannot believe . . . I mean . . . it is my sister . . . how does she come to be here?" Lord Henry said in bewilderment.

"Well, I think it must be because of the letter I wrote to her," Robert confessed. "On that first day, you seemed . . . it looked as though . . . er . . . you might not come through the experience, so I wrote to your sister. I thought someone of your family should know in case . . . well, I am sorry, sir, but I'm afraid it just went out of my head after that, and I forgot to inform you that I had written."

"Pray do not apologize for such good service, sir. I am too beholden to you to ever thank you enough as it is. It was only the surprise. Lizzie, my dear, are you feeling better?"

This as his sister's eyelids fluttered, closed, then opened to look up dazedly into all the faces bent over her own. "Do not call me Lizzie, Henry, you know I do not like it," came the reply, surprisingly strong for one who had just fainted so profoundly.

"Dear Lizzie, how like you," Henry laughed. "Come, let us help you to some place more comfortable than the floor. Robert, if you could . . ."

Robert came to her other side, and together they raised her to her feet and assisted her to the nearest chair, which was at the table in the breakfast room, the rest of the party following to resume their seats.

"Should she not lie down for a time? I could have a room made ready for her at once," India said, still hovering. "Or at least let us help her into the drawing room so that she may rest upon a sofa."

"Thank you," Henry's sister said, "but I shall do very well here, if I could just have a cup of coffee. No, no, I shall not need any hartshorn, thank you," she said, waving away the approaching footman bearing this concoction. "You may introduce me, if you please, Henry."

"This is my sister, Lady Elizabeth McFarland. And here are Lord and Lady Swanson, the dowager Lady Swanson, Lady Ursula Liddiard, and Miss Blanche Vernon, Lord Swanson's cousin," Henry said.

Lady Elizabeth nodded to each in turn. "Lord Swanson, I thank you for your letter. I left the same day I received it and have been on the road ever since. I apologize for my unseemly entrance, but you may imagine my feelings. Ten days on the road, every moment in agonizing worry, not certain if I would even arrive before he had breathed his last, and then to find him sitting up to table making a hearty breakfast, laughing, the picture of health! Well, it was enough and too much for me, though I have never suffered from a frail constitution."

"Dear madam, of course!" India cried. "How very harrowing such a journey must have been for you."

"But, Lizzie, where is Brian? Never tell me he let you travel here alone?"

"He was in Aran and there was no time to write to him—or so I thought. I have my abigail, and there were the coachman and two postilions to protect us. I left a note for Brian."

"I did write to you again four days later to tell you he had improved, but of course you had left by then, so you could not know," Robert said apologetically.

"Oh, yes, within the hour," Lady Elizabeth said cheerfully. "The maids packed, I ordered the traveling carriage, wrote my note to Brian, kissed the bairns, and we were off. The roads were quite dreadful in places, or we should have arrived sooner, but we had good fortune with the inns, except for one where the beds had not been aired properly."

"You must be exhausted," India said.

"Oh, no . . . but I am very hungry. I breakfasted at six, you see, to make an early start. Perhaps I might have some of that ham I see on the sideboard. And some baked eggs would be nice."

The eggs were ordered and the ham sliced and placed before her. She fell upon it with great appetite. She was not more than five feet tall, and though not fat, was well-rounded in figure. She was a very well-looking lady, her features and coloring very like her brother's, though clearly his elder sister.

India excused herself and bustled off to order a room to be made ready for Lady Elizabeth and to ensure that beds and food were found for her servants. Really, she thought happily, for she loved company, we are becoming a quite large party. After consulting with Cook about dinner, she returned to find Lord Henry just leaving the breakfast room with his sister on his arm.

"Ah, Lady Elizabeth, your room will be ready by now, if you should care to lie down for a time," India said.

"Good Lord, no, though I thank you. I never lie down in daylight, but I should go up and see that Tolly has unpacked my things properly. I will take my brother with me, if you won't mind, for a chat to catch up on family matters."

"Of course, you must both long to be private. Do go straight up."

Ursula came out then and said that Blanche and her aunt had gone up to Blanche's room. "And since it has come on to rain, I shall go up and write to Rupert and Albinia. Unless there is something I can do for you, India?"

"Nothing at all, dearest. Go along, and I'll come up and join you later, if I may."

Lady Elizabeth had gone up and soon was briskly ordering her maid in the disposal of various garments before dismissing her. She then sat down and ordered her brother to do the same. "Now, Henry, you must tell me all about everything. Where you were going, how you came to be on that road, what has happened to your horse—everything.''

Henry obediently sat down and succinctly recited his sorry tale: his fall, his rescue by Lady Ursula, his present state of health.

''Do you mean to tell me that young woman kept you from bleeding to death?''

''Well, I don't know that I would have quite bled to death, but she certainly staunched the wound with her petticoat, or at least so Robert claims—said I had an alluring bit of lace ruffle over one eye when they carried me in here. And God knows how much more serious things might have been for me if she had not acted with such dispatch.''

''That would be the young woman with the remarkable blue eyes, I hope. I was still somewhat fuzzy at the introductions. Probably because I was famished—my fainting, I mean. Goodness, how stupid that was. Why, I have never fainted in my life. Remarkable sensation, I must say, you feel so . . .''

''Why do you hope it was?''

''Hope what was?''

''That it was the young woman with the blue eyes?''

''Because I did not take to the blond young woman. She has a calculating look about her. On the lookout for a husband, I'll be bound, and you fill the bill remarkably well. But I shall never give my approval for such a match, Henry, so do not expect it.''

''Whoa up, sister, how you do rush your fences. Why are you suddenly talking of matrimony?''

''Because it is more than time for you to be thinking of it,'' she replied tartly, ''and I was only warning you of your danger. You know your taste for willowy blonds. I remember that Chaist person, for instance.''

''There is no danger at all in the direction of this particular willowy blond, I assure you,'' her brother replied firmly. ''Now, how are my godson and the rest of your brood?''

Dinner that evening was immensely enliv_____ ___
presence of Lady Elizabeth, who told them all ___
darling Brian and her four little boys, as well as the sta___
frank news that she would be blessed with another in a___ __
eight months.

"And this time I pray for a girl. Boys, of course, are necessary to carry on the name, but four are more than enough. I want daughters now. Have you a preference, Lady Swanson?"

India blushed and said she had none. Robert declared that he too would like a daughter, at which statement his mother bridled.

"Nonsense, Robert, you must have a son, of course. The firstborn should be a son, and I feel sure dear India will not disappoint us."

"Dear India could never disappoint *me*, Mama," Robert returned firmly.

India intervened hastily. "Where in Scotland do you live, Lady Elizabeth?"

"Up near Strathaven. About as far north as you can get."

"The winters must be dreadful!" the dowager shivered distastefully.

"It is very healthful. I am happy to say none of my bairns has ever had so much as a cold."

"Bairns, Lizzie? How Gaelic you are becoming," Henry teased.

"After seven years there, I would be bound to pick up the odd word here and there," Lady Elizabeth replied, "and I wish you will not call me Lizzie, Henry. You know I do not like it."

After dinner the ladies retired to the drawing room. There Blanche sat down beside Lady Elizabeth upon a sofa, prepared to charm her.

"I do hope you will make a long visit, Lady Elizabeth. You are such an amusing conversationalist."

"Amusing? I had no intention of being so. Perhaps you

mean you find my way of speaking amusing to you?''

"Oh, certainly not. I mean . . .'' Blanche halted in confusion, not really knowing how to escape the pit she saw yawning before her.

"Never mind. It does not matter. Oh, Lady Ursula, could we speak for a moment? You will excuse us, will you not, Miss . . . er . . . Vernon?''

Thus summarily dismissed, Blanche had nothing to do but remove herself, her mind boiling with frustration and humiliation.

Ursula came as she was bidden and sat down next to Lady Elizabeth, who said, "Now, my dear, I must first tell you of my heartfelt gratitude for all your courage and quick-wittedness in saving my brother.''

"Please do not credit me for more than being the first upon the scene, Lady Elizabeth. Anyone who came along at the time would have done as much as or perhaps more than I was able to do. And fortunately, I had my three servants, who helped me in everything.''

"I shall seek them out tomorrow, have no fear, but you must not be too modest, my dear. Another woman might have lost her wits or fainted, neither of which would have been of any use at all to my brother at the time. No, no, you must allow us to be grateful to you and tell you of it.''

"You are too kind. We are all so happy at his rapid recovery. Truly, at first it looked so very bad.''

"Please tell me all about it.''

"But surely Lord Henry has told you everything himself by now.''

"Pooh! He was unconscious through the most interesting part, and so could tell me nothing of it. I want the story in every detail from the one person who was there from the beginning.''

When the gentlemen came in, Ursula was giving Lady Elizabeth an edited version of Lord Henry's first awakening.

She halted abruptly as she saw Lord Henry coming purposefully across the room toward her.

"Well, ladies, shall we follow our usual practice of a stroll on the terrace?" he said.

Blanche jumped to her feet and said enthusiastically, "Just the thing I was longing for, Lord Henry. Shall we go out?" She came up and put her hand upon his arm expectantly.

"Not I, Henry," Lady Elizabeth said, "but do you go, Lady Ursula. I want to have a nice coze with Lady Swanson about babies."

Ursula rose and put her hand upon the arm Lord Henry was holding out to her, and the three walked out through the open French doors. Robert settled down with a London paper, and the dowager found a seat near a large candelabrum and took out her needlework.

"Now, Lady Swanson, please tell me all about that admirable young woman, Lady Ursula," Lady Elizabeth said.

13

"Well, Lord Swanson, if you can mount me, I shall ride today, since the sun shines," Lady Elizabeth declared the next morning.

"With the utmost pleasure, dear lady. I think I have just such a mount as will suit you."

"Oh, Lady Elizabeth, do you think it wise, in your . . . er . . . state of health?" the dowager asked.

"I am in very fine fettle today, thank you. The swoon yesterday was only from hunger, I do believe."

"Oh, I did not mean that. I referred to your . . . ah . . . expectations," the dowager explained delicately.

"Good Lord, do you mean because I am increasing? Pooh, nonsense, I rode for the first four months with each of the boys, and came to no harm, nor did they."

Henry came in then, looking gloomy. "Sorry to be late. It was the doctor. Dreadful old fusspot. Would not hear of my riding. I told him I should go mad if I could not exercise. He told me to take a walk. A walk!"

"Oh, poor Lord Henry! Shall I stay and keep you company in your walk?" Blanche cried.

"Good heavens, no! I mean . . . you would be mad to give up a ride for a walk," Henry protested with a hunted expression.

"And not the least need, Blanche," Robert said. "Henry shall come with me. I've to go to Cray's farm today. It will just about do you, Henry. One hour there, one hour back."

"There, now, Henry. A good tramp will be most beneficial. So do stop moping and eat a good breakfast," his sister said.

Blanche looked disgruntled for a moment, but realized this might not make such a good impression upon Lord Henry or his sister, and turned to her breakfast with a bright look and a smile all around to display her amiable disposition.

After breakfast, the day remaining clear, Ursula, Lady Elizabeth, and Blanche went up to change into riding costumes, and soon Sir Tarquin arrived with his sisters and they all went off down the drive. Henry and Robert set off briskly for Cray's farm, India sent for Cook to plan the day's menu, and the dowager settled down in her room to write letters. By the time she had finished, she heard India come upstairs and felt it was time to go down to the kitchen to meddle as usual with India's arrangements for dinner.

Presently India came down to the drawing room with her work basket to await the return of the riding party, and was joined there by her mother-in-law and, after an hour, by Robert and Henry, both looking very much better for their walk. India ordered wine and biscuits brought in.

As soon as the riding party reached the long path through the trees where they always went, Lady Elizabeth set her horse into a gallop. After a moment's indecision, Sir Tarquin went after her, the rest following along at a more moderate pace. Lady Elizabeth was too well-bred to go completely out of sight of the rest of her party with the only gentleman in attendance, and soon they came galloping back again.

"Ah, that was good—blew all the cobwebs away for sure," Lady Elizabeth cried with a breathless laugh as they wheeled around the rest and fell in behind. After she had caught her breath, she pressed forward to ride beside Ursula. Blanche immediately fell back to Sir Tarquin's side.

"Well, dear Lady Ursula, I congratulate you upon your fine seat. I do like to see a lady who knows how to sit upon a horse properly," Lady Elizabeth said.

"Very kind," Ursula murmured, turning pink with pleasure.

"I hear that you have been nursing your mother for several years. I hope you will not mind my asking, but was there no one else who could do so? No brothers or sisters?"

"Well, yes, there are a brother and two older sisters, but all of them have their own families to attend to."

"I hardly find that an acceptable excuse, unless you tell me the children had no nannies to attend to them."

"Well, actually . . . It was not only that . . . It is difficult to . . . you see, my mother was not easy to . . . to take care of."

"I see. They did not care to be bothered."

"Oh, not at all, but my mother would not allow them to do so . . ." She halted in confusion. It was difficult to be truthful about her dead mother's terrible disposition to a stranger.

"You mean she thought it was unnecessary since she still had an unmarried daughter at home. I fear I cannot condone such thinking. It might have been all right if you had already been on the shelf, but a young girl in the very first flush of youth, to be immured in a sickroom all those years? No, I say, no indeed. I cannot agree, and I think it was extremely selfish of your sisters to allow it."

Now Ursula was in a quandary. She did not like to hear her sisters, both good, kindly women, maligned, but to defend them she must expose more of her mother's character than she felt it was proper to do. Still, her mother was dead, and could take no harm, while Lady Elizabeth, who seemed of a forthright character, might say something slighting to an acquaintance about Ursula's sisters and tarnish their blameless reputations.

"It was not exactly that way, Lady Elizabeth. My sisters wrote many times offering to relieve me, they even came to try to do so, but . . . but my mother would not allow them near her. She was of a . . . a fretful disposition, you see, and could not bear anyone else to . . . I was the only one she could bear in her room.''

"I see," Lady Elizabeth said grimly. And indeed she did see—a young woman of calm disposition, who was biddable and who had too much compassionate understanding of her mother's suffering to ever show any resentment of her treatment. No wonder her mother kept her by her. Who else would put up with her sharp tongue? Lady Ursula might be too nice to say so, but that was how Lady Elizabeth interpreted "fretful disposition."

However, Lady Elizabeth was happy to note that the girl was no hypocrite, for there might be understanding of her mother and pity, but no love, for she wore no mourning and there was no pretense of grief. Lady Elizabeth silently applauded the courage it must take to refuse to bow to convention in these matters. A lot of spine there, she thought approvingly.

"And what are your plans now? Will you make your home with your brother or one of your sisters?"

"Not if I can think of something else," Ursula responded promptly, with a laugh. "Actually, I have not given much thought to the future as yet. I came straight here as soon as possible. India and I are bosom bows, you see, in fact she is my only friend. I've had no opportunity to make others. She has been begging me to come to her anytime these past six years—so I came. She is so good to me, and dear Robert . . . so kind. I mean to make a long visit, as I know she expects me to. In the meantime, I shall give thought to what I shall do about my future. I am five-and-twenty now and well able to take care of myself, and have fortunately some money of my own left me by my godmother, so I can be as independent as I like."

"A very sound approach to planning," Lady Elizabeth said. "Perhaps I could persuade you to come to me for a visit someday?" Ursula looked startled at this unexpected invitation. "Oh, no," Lady Elizabeth said with a laugh, "not all the way to Strathaven. That would be asking too much of anyone. But we do have the London house, and go there in the late spring for a few weeks—or for as long as I can persuade Brian to stay. Since I am so near, I shall probably go there for a time before I go back up north.''

"Your husband dislikes London?''

"He dislikes anyplace that isn't Strathaven. But we must go down at least once a year, for the dentist, and Brian must talk to his attorneys and so forth. I go for the parties and the opera and to see old friends. The bairns enjoy it immensely also. Then we're all very happy to get home again.''

"It sounds a wonderful life, Lady Elizabeth,'' Ursula said wistfully, remembering her sharp-tongued mother, who scorned caresses, and her rakish father, who was rarely at home.

Lady Elizabeth, whose heart was very soft, was touched by her words and impulsively laid her hand over Ursula's, folded together on her pommel. "I feel sure such a life is in store for you, dear girl,'' she said warmly.

"Ah, I would that I could believe you,'' Ursula said lightly.

"But of course it is. When you have rested up from your long ordeal and go about more, you will be bound to receive offers. Indeed, I feel sure you have had offers already. Is it not so?''

"Oh, indeed it is. Not three years ago. A Lord Batesley, do you know him?''

"Batesly? No, I don't believe he has come my way. Did your family object?''

"No indeed. At least, my mother was too ill to be consulted, but my brother was eager for the match. Lord Batesly is from a very old family and fabulously wealthy. There was only one flaw,'' she said sadly.

"Oh, dear, a flaw? What was it, my dear?''

"He was at least seventy years old. He had three wisps

of white hair, four teeth, and gout. Somehow, I just did not feel we would deal together.''

Lady Elizabeth gave a shout of laughter and Ursula joined in, causing the rest to look interested.

"Hi," Sir Tarquin called, "share the joke, do!"

"Oh, dear me, no, Sir Tarquin. We could not possibly," Lady Elizabeth said. "We women must be allowed our secrets, you know."

He had edged a little forward as he spoke, and Lady Elizabeth obligingly fell back next to Blanche. He happily rode forward to Ursula's side, and Lady Elizabeth watched interestedly as he began talking eagerly to her. They were certainly easy in each other's company, and if Lady Ursula wished, she could probably effect an offer from the gentleman at any time she chose, she thought with satisfaction for the girl's sake.

Sir Tarquin spoke rather plaintively to Ursula as they rode along together. "Dear Lady Ursula, I seem never to have any time alone with you anymore. Is all London determined to visit the Youngreaves this summer?"

She laughed. "Good heavens, sir, there are only three other guests."

"It seems like many more. And Lord Henry behaves as though your rescue of him entitles him to sole rights to your company."

"Now, really, Sir Tarquin, you must not say such things," she protested, hoping she would not blush.

"Well, he certainly would not let me get near enough to say two words to you last night," he grumbled. "I suppose any day now I shall find him along on our morning rides."

"I am sure I hope you may be right, sir, for that would mean he has fully recovered, and I feel sure you would not begrudge him good health."

"There is only one thing I begrudge him, and that is the time he spends in your company," he said with an ardent look at her. "I wish I had been the one to fall on my head and be rescued by you."

She could not help laughing at this absurdity, but he looked hurt and said, "I wish you will take me seriously, dear Lady Ursula, for I *am* serious, I assure you."

"Oh, that will never do, sir. One must never be serious on such a glorious day as this."

He reached out and caught up her hand and pulled it toward his lips, but she snatched it away with a fearful look behind. Reassured that no one seemed to be watching them, she turned back and gave him a reproving look before slowing down and allowing the others to catch up to them. For the remainder of the ride she made sure they rode very near the others to prevent any more *tête-à-têtes*. She had thought their little flirtation was in the spirit of friendliness and fun. She did not want it to become more than that.

They came out of the forest path onto the road and very soon were back to Swan Court, where they were welcomed by the stay-at-homes. Sir Tarquin was again urged to come back for dinner and gladly accepted.

India hurriedly sent off notes to Mr. Phillips-Glenn-Phillips and the vicar, telling the footman to wait for replies, and was gratified within the hour to receive their acceptances.

That evening Blanche was again resplendent in seafoam green with Brussels lace. Is there no end to her wardrobe? Ursula wondered. She herself wore a simple lemon sarcenet. Robert took in Lady Elizabeth, Henry led in Ursula, and Sir Tarquin the dowager, followed by Blanche with Mr. Phillips-Glenn-Phillips, and India with the vicar. At table Robert had Lady Elizabeth on his right, with the vicar next to her; then came the dowager and Sir Tarquin on India's left. Henry was on her right, next to Blanche. Mr. Phillips-Glenn-Phillips sat on her other side, next to Ursula on Robert's left. Tonight Blanche looked more than pleased with her position. She began to talk with great animation to Lord Henry. In fact the whole party was animated, mostly owing to the vicar, who had a fund of witty stories about the foolishness of some of his parishioners, and Lady Elizabeth, who could be counted upon to offer funny comments upon his stories, and from time to time offer a few Highland stories, complete with appropriate Scottish accent.

Lord Henry had no difficulty at all in foiling Blanche's attempts to monopolize him. He listened attentively, laughed at her quips, but turned easily to India when Blanche had, perforce, to attend to her plate, or sometimes spoke down the table to his sister about some hilarious episode from one of his visits to Strathaven. The rallies between them were frequent and sometimes lengthy and amused the entire company with the exception of Blanche. Despite her knowledge that it was not becoming to show her displeasure openly, she could not help pouting that Henry should want to talk so incessantly to his own sister. As for India, she was married, for heaven's sake. Of course he must be polite to her as his hostess, but need he be so quite so often? Here he was, seated beside the most beautiful girl at the table, who also had wit and the art of flirtation down to perfection, and he could neglect her to talk to his sister!

After dinner, when the gentlemen rejoined them, Henry went straight to the sofa where Ursula sat with his sister, and pulling up a chair, sat down to talk. After a time he suggested that Lady Elizabeth give them some music, and she agreed amiably, rising at once to go across to the pianoforte without any fuss.

It was clear at once that she had a great deal of talent, and played several light pieces by Mozart and Beethoven with brilliance. She played an encore without demur when it was demanded, clearly enjoying herself, and then called her brother to come and sing. He obliged, and sang several tender German lieder in a surprisingly true tenor voice.

Sir Tarquin moved over to seat himself next to Ursula, but she hushed him when he tried to speak while the music was playing. Blanche looked at them, her mouth tight with anger for a moment, but then turned about and concentrated her full attention upon Lord Henry.

When he finished, India called upon Sir Tarquin to perform for them, saying she knew he sang well because his sisters had told her so. He at first demurred, but India persisted and he at last obliged with several Spanish songs he had learned in his travels.

By the time he had finished, the tea tray was brought in, and over it Sir Tarquin put forth a proposal. "I wonder if I could persuade all of you to come to me tomorrow. My mama and sisters would be delighted. My sisters are not out yet, so Mama does not allow them to go out to parties, so they are always begging for entertainments at home," he declared with all the confidence of a young man whose womenfolk make of him their idol, and with none of the knowledge as to what work would be demanded of them when they learned they were to entertain nine visitors to dinner on the following evening.

"Sounds like a good idea to me," Robert said.

"It would be very nice indeed, Sir Tarquin, and we should be happy to come," India said, "though perhaps . . . do you think you should consult first with your mother?"

"Oh, no, indeed, she will be delighted, I assure you," the idol said.

Everyone made sounds of pleasure, particularly Mr. Phillips-Glenn-Phillips and the vicar, who, being middle-aged bachelors, were always delighted to be asked out anywhere, especially to dinner.

14

Lady Rochdale had risen to the occasion magnificently. After the shock of her son's casual announcement upon his arrival home that he had invited nine guests for dinner on the following evening, she had sat in stunned silence for a moment, but rallied almost at once. It was, after all, darling Tarquin's home and he was free to invite anyone to it that he cared to. Her mind went instantly to work on menus: could the fishmonger supply her with lobster? was her first thought, followed by other dishes, then what gowns her daughters would wear, which flowers she would order the gardener to bring into the house, and what gentlemen she could call upon at such short notice to make up her table—sixteen people! Goodness, she would have her work cut out for her tomorrow, but it was worth it for dear Tarquin, bless him.

Despite her quite frenzied day of preparations for this large entertainment, Lady Rochdale stood with serene dignity in purple-bloom silk, a pretty daughter in fresh white muslin and a string of seed pearls on either side of her, to receive the party from Swan Court. Earlier arrivals, including the vicar, Mr. Phillips-Glenn-Phillips, Mr. Bracegood, a local squire, and his twenty-year-old twin sons, George and John, were disposed about the room. Sir Tarquin was at the door to greet his guests as they entered. He led Ursula up to his mother to be introduced with all the triumphant pride of a dog laying a bone at his master's feet. Lady Rochdale grasped the situation at once and made a great fuss over Ursula.

Introductions were made all around, and everyone being pleased to be there and of cheerful disposition, there was soon a hum of conversation rising pleasantly upon the air. Blanche, conscious of being the most modishly dressed woman in the room, was in very good spirits and was dazzling the Bracegood twins with her rich figured-white-French-gauze-over-satin gown and her flirtatious conversation.

Ursula felt quite cast in the shade, though she wore her absolute favorite gown, saved for an occasion like this, of blue-violet silk, which almost exactly matched her eyes. The high-waisted gown was cut low, exposing a very pretty bosom, had short puffed sleeves, and was embellished only with a silver ribbon tied just under the bosom, with the long ends fluttering down to the hem of the narrow skirt. India watched her dotingly and thought her ravishing, and noted that Sir Tarquin could hardly take his eyes from her. Other eyes followed, she saw, for Lord Henry, engaged in conversation with his hostess and the vicar, managed not to lose sight of her.

Still chatting gaily, the whole company trooped in to dinner when it was announced. Blanche was gratified to find herself seated between Henry and George Bracegood, and settled to her dinner with good appetite and lively wit. It was unfortunate that Sir Tarquin sat at the other end of the table and was out of her reach, but she would certainly find the opportunity after dinner to further her campaign to trap him into a declaration. Not that she meant to accept him while Lord Henry was available, but it never hurt to have two strings to one's bow.

Lady Rochdale's cook had outdone herself, with two complete courses and at least three removes in each, including turtle soup, green goose with French beans and mushrooms, removed by tenderloin of veal with truffles. In the second course, an escallop of oysters was removed by

a dressed lobster, followed by fillets of turbot in an Italian
sauce. Then came a Savoy cake and several creams and
jellies.

The company became almost sommolent toward the end
of this filling repast, and the ladies were happy to leave the
gentlemen at last for the more comfortable seating of the
drawing room, where they had plenty of time to recover,
since the men were discinclined to move from their port for
nearly three-quarters of an hour.

When they did come into the drawing room, Miss Rochdale
and Miss Anne began pleading with their mama for some
dancing, claiming a great need for exercise after all that food,
and when the Bracegood twins seconded the idea enthusiastically, Lady Rochdale good-naturedly consented and rang
for the servants to roll back the rugs and push back the
furniture in the second drawing room, a good-sized apartment
opening out of the main drawing room.

"But you know, my dears, I am not very good at the
pianoforte for dancing, and we must have music," she said.

"Oh, dear Blanche is a most accompanied performer,"
the dowager gushed, always eager to cry her niece's talents.

"I do not play that sort of music," Blanche said firmly,
with a quelling look at her aunt for thinking she, Blanche,
would be willing to be stuck at the piano like an old spinster
aunt while there was dancing going forward.

"I think I am quite proficient enough," Ursula said, "so
if you will help me look out some music, we can begin at
once."

"Oh, no, darling, you—" India began in dismay.

"Oh, yes," Ursula replied, taking India's arm and leading
her toward the pianoforte. "Now, come along and help us
choose the music." As they went, she murmured quietly,
"I do not dance tonight, dear one."

"But you must . . . you should . . ." India protested.

"No, no. I may not be in mourning and I do not grieve,

but I cannot dance on my mother's grave. It would be most improper, darling. She has not been dead a month. Surely you must agree.''

India said no more, for what could she say? She knew very well that Ursula was right. It was only that in the press of events since her arrival, India had forgotten the reason Ursula had at last been able to come for a visit. Also she remembered Ursula as a most accomplished dancer and longed to show her off to the company.

A set was formed for some country dances. Lord Henry led out the elder Rochdale daughter after Lady Rochdale had laughingly refused his request to stand up with her. Tarquin bowed before Lady Elizabeth, while George Bracegood led out Blanche and his brother partnered Miss Anne Rochdale. Robert pulled his wife into the set, though she protested, and the rest declared they would watch, for the country dances were too lively for their health after such a satisfying dinner.

Blanche was resentful to be relegated to a green squire's son, for surely at this rustic affair there could be no doubt as to her status as belle of the ball. Of course she knew well that Lord Henry must offer his hostess the first dance, or if not her, her elder daughter, and likewise, Sir Tarquin's duty demanded that he lead out Lady Elizabeth, who took precedence over every other woman there as the daughter of a duke and the wife of an earl. Nevertheless, it rankled in Blanche's mind even while she turned her charm upon an already bemused George Bracegood, who could not believe his good fortune in being flirted with by a regular London out-and-outer.

In the next set, a quadrille, Blanche was mollified by seeing Lord Henry bowing before her. Sir Tarquin was hanging over Ursula at the pianoforte, evidently not intending to dance this set at all. Blanche rose with what she thought of as a proper languor to accept Lord Henry's hand, bent on demonstrating to everyone that she was quite used to being importuned by handsome young gentlemen to favor them with a dance.

"How kind of you, Lord Henry, to ask Miss Rochdale to dance the first set, though I fear you may have turned her head."

"Oh? How is that, Miss Vernon?"

"Well, she will not realize that it was your duty, and may place too much importance upon it. These young country girls, you know, have no experience of how the *ton* behaves."

"Oh, I shouldn't place too much faith in that view, Miss Vernon. It seems to me she is enjoying herself with young Bracegood much more than she did with me."

Blanche laughed heartily at such a possibility, causing Ursula to glance up from the music. The sight of such a handsome couple so much in charity with one another for some reason caused a mantle of depression to settle upon her. Blanche, with her beautiful wardrobe and her town bronze, must surely be a more likely companion to the sophisticated Lord Henry than anyone else in the room, and Blanche did want a husband so badly. These charitable thoughts did nothing at all to dispel her gloom.

Sir Tarquin noticed her change of expression and bent solicitously over her to inquire if she were tired of playing.

"Oh, no, no indeed, Sir Tarquin. I am enjoying it very much and I do love to see people having a good time."

"I would much prefer you to be enjoying yourself," he said softly.

"But I tell you I am doing so."

"I meant I would rather have you dance than play for others to do so."

"You must know I cannot dance yet, Sir Tarquin, though I too would find it preferable."

"I will live for the day when I may lead you out," he said fervently, with such a meaningful smile that she blushed and looked away, to find herself staring straight into Lord Henry's eyes. She hastily turned her own back to the music and did not see Lord Henry's brows drawn together in a frown.

"Oh, dear, Lord Henry," said Blanche, who had seen it, "have you become quite fatigued with all this dancing? Perhaps we could sit out upon the terrace while you recruit your strength."

"Not at all, Miss Vernon. I hope I am not still considered an invalid, for I am fully recovered, I assure you."

By the end of the evening, Lord Henry had stood up three times with Blanche and Ursula had the headache. She was very glad to be handed into Robert's carriage, even though she had to endure the ride home listening to Blanche and the dowager recounting Blanche's triumphs all the way.

Morning, however, brought a lifting of the headache as well as her spirits, especially when she went down to breakfast to find that Blanche was having another lie-in and would not be down this morning. When she had eaten, Ursula went up to change, and came down to find Lord Henry just coming around the house astride the horse his friend Poynton had so thoughtfully sent for his use, and leading the mare Robert had designated as Ursula's.

He leapt down at once and came to toss her up into the saddle, just as the Rochdale party came clattering up the drive. Sir Tarquin frowned, but then said a cheery good morning, managing to hide his displeasure. He dismounted and went to assist Lady Elizabeth, who had just come out, into her saddle.

"Good heavens, Lord Henry, has the doctor relented at last?" Miss Rochdale cried.

"No, though I am sure he would have if I had been able to ask him."

Blanche heard the party leaving and rose to dress in a most becoming moss-green muslin, much flounced about the hem, and descended presently to the study. It was, however, empty but for Robert going over some papers. He looked up and frowned at her, and she retreated hastily. Having checked the drawing room, also empty, she sought out her aunt.

"Has Lord Henry been kept in bed today?" she demanded peremptorily as she flung open the door to her aunt's bedroom.

"Laws, child, how you startled me! I have not seen anyone this morning, for I did not go down to breakfast when I learned that you—"

"Well, go then and find out," Blanche interrupted with barely suppressed impatience.

The dowager hurried off and returned in not more than three minutes with the news that Lord Henry had just been seen by Crigly riding down the drive with the regular morning party.

Blanche picked up her aunt's hairbrush and dashed it into the fireplace, denting the silver back, before storming off to her own room. With the help of Botts she donned her habit and ran out to the stables to demand a mount.

"There be nothing fit to ride left now, my lady," said the stableman.

"Why, then, what is that?" she asked haughtily, pointing with her riding crop at a fine bay, rolling an eye at her nervously over the top of his stall door.

"Her be spavined," the stableman replied succinctly.

"And that one?"

"That be m'lord's."

"Then I'll have him. Saddle him at once."

"Beggin' pardon, m'lady, but that do be Lord Robert's own mount, ordered by him for half-hour from now."

"I am sure my cousin will not mind if I ride it. Saddle it."

"So and I will, m'lady, just so soon as he'm tell me to do so hisself," the stableman said flatly.

Blanche stood irresolutely, trembling with frustration and fury, before turning on her heel and leaving the yard. She knew it was pointless to ask Robert to let her have his horse, so there was nothing for her to do but return to the house and change again. She relieved her feelings by boxing Botts's ear when that person dared to ask if she had changed her mind about riding today.

How could the fates have been so unkind to her? Why was she balked in this way when so much depended upon it? After his attentiveness to her the evening before, how could Lord Henry not have told her of his intention to ride today? Surely if he was beginning to develop a *tendre* for her, he would have made sure of her company this morning.

She paced up and down the room, kicking at the furniture and demanding that Botts stop sniveling and get on with her work. She would have loved to throw something again, but was too careful of her own things to mistreat them.

Ursula's heart had behaved in a strangely disturbing way as she saw Lord Henry riding toward her, leading her mare. She felt breathless and almost mindless for a moment, but the almost immediate arrival of the Rochdales, as well as Lady Elizabeth's appearance from the house, forced her to pull her wits together. The party was enlarged today by the addition of the Bracegood twins, who looked quite cast down when they saw that Miss Vernon was not to be one of the party.

Under cover of the general conversation that ensued as they went down the drive, Ursula had time to examine what had happened to her and had no difficulty in arriving at the correct conclusion. She had unknowingly allowed herself to begin forming an attachment that was clearly doomed to cause only heartache in the future. It would never do! She was extremely vexed with herself and determined that as of this moment she would be very much on her guard with him and with her thoughts of him. She had always congratulated herself upon being of so practical a set of mind that she had never suffered from the foolish starts and infatuations of other young girls, and had no intention of having to admit to herself so lowering a thought as that she was now going to behave so.

As a consequence, she spent most of the ride talking with Sir Tarquin, who was much gratified by her obvious preference for his company. Lady Elizabeth took note that her brother eyed the couple with no evidence of pleasure. She would have liked very much to know her brother's true feelings, but realized that now was not the time to probe them.

He was remembering that moment the evening before when he had caught her eye as Sir Tarquin stood bending over her, whispering into her ear as she played, and how, when she saw him watching, she had blushed and looked away. He remembered also her startled expression when he had brought around her mare. Had she been disappointed that Sir Tarquin, already coming up the drive, had not been there soon enough to assist her into the saddle as usual?

His brows drew together in a frown, and he looked away from the couple riding so companionably together before him to meet his sister's speculative gaze. He looked away hastily and dropped back to ride beside Miss Rochdale.

15

On the next morning it was a very good thing that Lady Elizabeth said she would not ride, for Blanche was determined to do so and would certainly have caused everyone some uncomfortable moments if she had been frustrated in her plans. She was glad to find that she had Lord Henry almost entirely to herself, for Ursula, having spent a sleepless hour or so the night before taking herself to task, was more resolved than ever to behave sensibly. She therefore was amiable and smiling to everyone, and engaged herself in conversation with the company at large as much as possible, though not avoiding any *tête-à-têtes* with Sir Tarquin.

The Bracegood twins, after having surrounded Blanche with their attentions at the start, soon found themselves, they knew not how, displaced by Lord Henry., Blanche was very clever at these sorts of manipulations and had no trouble at all in acquiring a position beside Lord Henry that she clung to for the entire ride.

Lady Elizabeth, when she at last came downstairs after writing a long and loving letter to her darling Brian and the bairns, found only the dowager ensconced in the drawing room with her tambour frame.

"Ah, dear Lady Elizabeth, I do hope you are not feeling ill?"

"Not the least in the world. I only wanted to write to my

husband or I should have ridden today as usual," Lady Elizabeth said heartily. "Does your niece ride today?"

"Oh, yes, indeed. She does hate to be left out of anything the other young people are doing."

"She is a pretty young woman. I am surprised at her being unmarried still."

"Ah, she has had many offers, of course. But I fear she is too refined in her tastes."

"No doubt. I find young women are not marrying so early these days. There is Lady Ursula, still single and so attractive. Of course, she has had little chance, with the burden of her mother all these years, poor child."

"Well, she is a pretty-behaved young woman, but has not the sort of looks or spirit that draws men to her, in my opinion."

"Oh, do you think so? I find her quite lovely. And Sir Tarquin seems to think so also."

"Oh, Sir Tarquin," the dowager said dismissively. "Indeed we are expecting him to make her an offer at any moment. He arrived back from the West Indies only a few days after Lady Ursula's own arrival here, and has been most attentive from the moment he clapped eyes on her."

"And does she return his feelings, do you think?"

"Most certainly I do. After all, she cannot really hope to do much better for herself. Not an heiress, you know, and no beauty. No, no fear, he will be glad to get an earl's daughter and she will be glad to take him. She seemed to form an attachment for him from the first, from what I have seen. The young are so impetuous, are they not? Now, I have noticed another romance blossoming," she added with a coy smirk.

"Indeed?"

"Oh, yes, our other young gentleman shows signs of falling in love with my darling Blanche."

"Do you mean one of the Bracegood boys?"

"Oh, good heavens, no! Though I don't doubt they would

either of them be eager enough if she gave them any encouragement. No, it was a gentleman much closer to you—and dear Blanche, though she tries to hide it, is already head over ears, I think.''

Lady Elizabeth realized with horror that the dowager was hinting at something between Henry and Blanche. She would warn Henry of it, to be sure, but it was the other news that she found somewhat less than thrilling. Of course, if Lady Ursula loved Sir Tarquin, and he her, there was nothing in the world to object to. However, the arrangement did not march with the ideas she had been forming in these past days. It had been her hope for some years now to see her brother married and settled in life. From her observations of him since her arrival, it had seemed that her hopes might at last be gratified, for it appeared that her brother was on the way to developing a *tendre* for Lady Ursula. What Lady Ursula's feelings for her brother were, she did not know, though she seemed on easy terms with him. The same, however, was true of her attitude to Sir Tarquin. Of course, Lady Ursula was too well-bred to betray herself with sighs or languishing glances.

What to do? Lady Elizabeth would have liked very much to sit down with the girl and probe the matter, but they were not on such terms of intimacy that made such a thing possible. However, she was on such terms with her brother. She would take the first opportunity to speak to him. If he did care for Lady Ursula, then he must set to work at once to fix his interest with her before Sir Tarquin beat him to it.

In this, though she could not know it, she was too late. Sir Tarquin, by challenging Ursula to a race, had drawn her nearly a mile away from the rest of the party. They were soon out of sight, and pointing to a tree as a goal, they galloped along furiously to draw up laughing and breathless, each claiming to have won.

He suggested they dismount for a while and allow the rest to catch up. She agreed, and they walked aside into a planta-

tion of trees. After only a moment, he stopped and turned
to her.

"Lady Ursula, will you allow me to speak to you about
something very much on my mind?"

"Why . . . I . . ." She faltered. "Yes, of course, Sir
Tarquin."

"It is of my feelings. In this short time that I have known
you, I have grown to love you so very much that I—"

"Oh, please do not go on, I beg of you," she cried, much
alarmed.

"You must allow me to speak, Lady Ursula . . . Ursula
. . . dearest Ursula," he cried, possessing himself of her
hands and drawing her close. "Please say you can return
my love. I will wait forever if you will only say you will
marry me."

She was so shocked that she could only stare at him for
a long moment while she ordered her senses. Then gently
she withdrew her hands from his and stepped back. "Dear
friend, this is indeed a great surprise to me. I am, of course,
aware of the great honor you do me, but it is not possible
for me to accept it."

"Oh, do not say so, darling girl, take all the time you
require to adjust to the idea, and I'm sure you will see how
well-attuned we two have been since our first meeting."

"Indeed, I do not require any time at all to see that, Sir
Tarquin. It has been a source of great satisfaction to me that
so very soon after I came here I was able to claim you and
your sisters as friends. It is always pleasing to have a fine
and honorable man for a friend, but alas, there cannot be
anything beyond that between us."

"Is there someone else? Is it Lord—?"

"There is no one," she interrupted him quickly and
emphatically. "I beg you not to pursue this matter further,
since to do so would force me to cause unhappiness for both
of us. Let us go on as we have and forget this episode. I
would be very grateful to always be able to call you friend."

"Can you not at least give me some hope that you will change your mind as you come to know me better?"

"No, Sir Tarquin, there can be no hope of that."

"No hope? How can that be? Surely if you—"

"No, dear friend. I will not be so dishonest as to profess that I have had no inkling that in the last week or so you have shown me something of your feelings. This has forced me to examine my own, and I have learned that I cannot feel that love that is your due—that I would want to feel for the man I marry, if indeed there is such a person. It would be horribly unfair to both of us to marry without that love, and most of all to you, who deserve to receive from your wife as much love as you will so generously give someday when you meet her. Please forgive me that I cannot be that person."

He looked at her despairingly, but the sounds of the rest of the party approaching caused him to square his shoulders and extend his arm to lead her back to their horses.

When they returned to Swan Court, India invited them all to come in for a light luncheon, and all accepted eagerly and fell upon the food with good appetite, except for Sir Tarquin, Lady Ursula, and Lord Henry, who all made only a token show of enjoying the meal.

Lady Elizabeth noticed that while Sir Tarquin seemed to be in a state of suppressed excitement, and Lady Ursula somewhat pensive, her brother was looking grim. Clearly something had occurred that morning to displease him. As they left the table, she asked him if he would care to come to her room at his convenience during the afternoon. He merely nodded his agreement and disappeared.

Though he kept her waiting for over an hour, Lady Elizabeth did not fret. Having said he would come, or at least nodded his acceptance, he would come. When his tap at the door came, she bade him enter. He closed the door behind him and trod across the floor to stand over her where she sat on a chaise longue beside the window.

"Well, Lizzie, you wanted to speak to me?"

She looked up at him towering over her. "Sit down, dearest, do, or I shall have a stiff neck," she said complainingly.

He hooked a chair forward with his foot and sat down, folded his arms across his chest, and waited for what she had to say with a singular lack of encouragement in his expression.

She surveyed him with some trepidation. "Well . . . it is so difficult to know exactly how to begin."

"Come, this from you, Lizzie? I have never known you at a loss for words."

"I wish you will not call me Lizzie," she said crossly. "And I should warn you that Miss Vernon is definitely setting her cap for you and is expecting a declaration at any moment."

"I have always called you so, and you never objected until you put up your hair and let down your skirts. As for Miss Vernon, I hope I have learned all there is to know about avoiding such traps as she sets. You may take my word for it that it is all some fantasy in her own head."

"I thought as much myself. She is not at all the sort of young woman I would—"

"Come along, Lizzie, you did not ask me here to tell me of Miss Vernon. Cut line and get it out."

"I was only wondering . . . It seems to me that I have noticed a certain . . . partiality developing in your feelings toward . . . a certain young woman."

"Good heavens! Such circumlocution. Are you to sit here mincing around your subject all afternoon?"

"I am not mincing!" she cried, stung. "I never mince."

"No, not as a rule. But now you are."

"Very well, if you want the truth, I am speaking of Lady Ursula."

"What about her?" he said unhelpfully.

"Now who is guilty of circumlocution? You know perfectly well what I mean."

"I do not care to discuss the matter just at present, Lizzie."

"No, of course you do not. You prefer to go on in a very slow-top sort of way until you finally make up your mind. Why must you make such a piece of work of it?"

His brows drew together awfully. "What are you talking about?"

"Only that you are so afraid to commit yourself to any permanency in your life. Men really disgust me! So afraid to give up your precious independence, so sure you have only to snap your fingers when you are ready and the bird will hop into your hand. Well, let me tell you it doesn't often work that way. In fact, very rarely."

"I fear you leave me still in the dark. I do not take your meaning. Certainly not as it applies to me."

"Please do not pretend to be so dense. I know you well enough to be sure you are awake in every suit. I am saying that if you do not make your intentions clear, you will find someone has been before you and the bird has flown."

"What is all this continuous reference to birds?" he demanded irritably.

"Very well. I will lay it out for you simply so that you will understand. Surely it cannot have escaped your notice that Sir Tarquin Rochdale is very particular in his attentions to Lady Ursula. I do not know whether she returns his feelings myself, but I have it on authority from one of this household that they are in almost hourly expectation of a proposal from him—and that they are in no doubt that when it comes she will accept him. Is that plain enough speaking for you?"

Scowling horribly, he rose and strode across to stare out the window, his back to her.

"Darling Henry, believe me, I know it is not to your liking that I interfere in your affairs in this way," she said imploringly, "but I think this would be such a good thing for you. I have never met a girl I liked so well or one I thought so well-suited for you. Indeed, nor one that I ever saw you showing such a proper regard for. I care very much for you and it is my fondest dream to see you happily married at last. Don't you see that in the circumstances it is imperative that you act quickly before it is too late?"

He did not speak for some time, seeing again Ursula, her hand upon Sir Tarquin's arm, emerging from the trees, their self-conscious air, her look of confusion as she glanced up and saw him approaching. There was no doubt in his mind that Sir Tarquin had just made her his declaration, and after the news he had just heard from his sister, that she had accepted him.

He turned to his sister. "I fear it is too late, my dear," he said bleakly, and quickly left the room.

That night, as she prepared for bed, a note from him informed her that he proposed leaving the house as early as it was convenient for her on the following morning, when he would be happy to escort her to London.

16

Naturally, Lady Elizabeth was very much put out by this missive, and pulling on a dressing gown, she hurried down the corridor to rap peremptorily upon his door.

He opened it to her himself, and scowled when he saw her. "What is it, Lizzie?"

"If I might come in. I prefer not to discuss this in the hallway."

He stared at her for a moment, but then reluctantly stood aside for her to enter. She wasted no time in coming to grips with him. "Henry, what is the meaning of this?" she demanded indignantly, waving his note before his nose. He snatched it from her and threw it into the fire.

"It seemed perfectly comprehensible to me. What was it that you did not understand?"

"You must be all about in your head if you think I can go to Lady Swanson in the morning and tell her we are leaving at once. Why, what can I possibly say to her as to our reason for such an abrupt departure?"

"Oh, say anything you like," he snapped irascibly.

"But it will be so rude! They cannot see it as anything but an insult after all their kindness to you—and to me as well. It is beyond anything I have ever heard of. It will be like a . . . a slap in the face, and they will never forgive either of us, and I can't blame them," Lady Elizabeth cried, nearly in tears.

"Oh, please do not enact me any Cheltenham tragedies,

143

Liz. I must leave here—at once. Say anything—say I have been having headaches and want to consult a physician in London at once. Say we will both write once we reach town. Say . . . oh, say anything, but I am leaving before midday tomorrow. I cannot stay to see . . . to learn . . .'' He turned away abruptly and stood staring down into the fire.

She felt her heart turn over with love and pity for him. Clearly he had seen or overheard something between Lady Ursula and Sir Tarquin to confirm the truth of what she had learned from the dowager. Clear also that he was being made intolerably unhappy by it. He was more smitten than she had believed possible for him, and could not stay to witness the couple's happiness while his own heart was breaking, all his hopes smashed.

"Very well, Henry. It shall be as you say," she said softly. "I will set Tolly packing now and speak to Lady Swanson first thing in the morning."

She returned to her room and ordered an astonished Tolly to pack the cases, as they would leave the next day. Having spent a troubled night, Lady Elizabeth ordered breakfast sent up to her. While she ate, Tolly did the last of the packing, then took a note from Lady Elizabeth to Lady Swanson respectfully requesting that lady to attend her in her room.

Blanche and Ursula went up at the same time to change for riding: Blanche, though he had not appeared for breakfast, certain that Lord Henry would be joining them, Ursula determined to prove to Sir Tarquin that all was the same between them.

India, in Lady Elizabeth's room, was learning the startling news that Lord Henry had sent for his sister in the night as he was suffering from a severe headache. Lady Elizabeth had then determined that her brother must be examined at once by London's leading physician. They both deplored this drastic move that cut short so pleasant a stay, but Elizabeth felt certain Lady Swanson would see the necessity for it.

India could only agree, expressing her horror that Lord

Henry should have suffered and praying that it would prove to be nothing serious. Lady Elizabeth promised to write at once with news of what the London doctor might say, and added profuse expressions of her eternal gratitude for all the kindness and care extended to her brother and herself.

All of this took some forty-five minutes, and in the meantime Ursula and Blanche had gone down to meet Sir Tarquin. Blanche's irritation at the nonappearance of Lord Henry knew no bounds. She felt that one day he was warm, the next indifferent. She simply could make no sense of his attitude at all. She tossed her head and began to flirt with Sir Tarquin. This made everything much easier for Ursula, though he seemed somewhat stiff in his greeting to her. As for Lord Henry, she spent some time persuading herself that it was much better that he was not with them today.

When they returned, India met Ursula in the hall and drew her aside into a small reception room to break the news to her that Lord Henry and his sister had departed half an hour previously for London to consult with a doctor there about Henry's violent headache during the night.

Ursula turned white and sank abruptly into a chair. "Headache! Oh, dear God, do you think his injury caused some serious damage to his brain?"

"I don't think anything of the sort! Please let us try not to jump to such dire conclusions. He had a bad headache and his sister determined to carry him off to London at once. It was only sensible for her to do so. I should have done the same in her place," India said firmly.

"But . . . but he was doing so well . . . he looked so well, and then to . . . to leave so suddenly without . . . without . . ."

"They were extremely sorry to leave without seeing you, and said everything that was proper to apologize, but they wanted as early a start as possible, hoping to reach London by tonight. They each left a note for you." She handed over the two missives and Ursula opened Henry's quickly.

Lord Henry was formal, thanking her again for all she had done for him, hoping he might be given the opportunity of someday repaying her, and remaining always her obedient servant. Ursula read the few lines through swiftly and then again more slowly and let her hand drop into her lap while she sat staring into space.

"Will you not read Lady Elizabeth's note?" India said after a time.

"What? Oh . . . to be sure." She opened it and read it, a very warm, friendly note that promised to write more fully from London. She handed both notes over to India, turning away to hide the tears that she could not suppress. India read them quickly and then came to sit beside her friend and pull her into her arms. At this, all Ursula's resolve to keep her hurt and disappointment to herself broke down and she cried into India's shoulder. India said nothing, asked no questions. Indeed, she had no need to do so, for she knew now what she had suspected and hoped for was true—only now she wished very much that she had never hoped for it.

Blanche, meanwhile, had learned the news from her excited aunt, all agog over the departure. Blanche immediately flew into a temper tantrum, followed by strong hysterics. The dowager fluttered around, waving her vinaigrette bottle beneath Blanche's nose until Blanche snatched it from her and hurled it at the fireplace, where it hit the fender and the delicate crystal shattered into pieces.

Blanche simply could not reconcile what she had begun to think of as a certain conquest with this abrupt departure, without so much as a hint of his intentions, not to speak of no word of good-bye, either in person or by note. Could she have been mistaken in her certainty that he was, slowly to be sure, developing a partiality for her? Or perhaps—yes—perhaps he had indeed begun to feel more for her than was acceptable to his long-established bachelorhood and gone sneaking off in this cowardly way. Oh, she raged, what despicable creatures men were! Her fingers itched to administer a resounding box to his ear.

The departing party would have been astonished that their leaving could have caused Blanche such violent emotions. They had no thoughts at all to spare for Blanche. Lady Elizabeth rode in her carriage with Tolly, while Henry's man, Archer, sat up beside the coachman. Henry rode the horse his friend had sent him. He had informed his sister that as they would be passing very near Poynton's place, they would stop there briefly to return his horse and thank him for his thoughtfulness, after which he would join his sister in the carriage for the remainder of the trip to London.

Lady Elizabeth sat silently, overcome with guilt at having returned the Youngreaves' kindness with lies and subterfuges. However, it had all been necessary for Henry's sake, and so she could only hope to be forgiven someday. She could not have told India the real reason for their departure, for that was Henry's business and not her place to discuss it. She wished, though, that she had asked young Lady Swanson about her mother-in-law's assertion regarding Lady Ursula and Sir Tarquin. She had not thought about it at the time. Never mind, when she reached London she would write to her and ask if there was news in that direction.

Henry rode along in a veritable miasma of gloom for the first time in his life. He who had flirted his way through Season after Season, party after party, and never come close to losing his heart. It had been his proud boast that he had never met a woman to whom he would be willing to be legshackled for the rest of his life, and furthermore had no intention of even looking about for a wife before he reached the age of forty. Time enough then for a man to settle down and set up his nursery, he said, when he had the years and experience to make a wise choice.

Yet here he was, barely thirty years old, with ten years of his pledge still to go, profoundly in love with a woman who had apparently given her heart away to another with no thought of him at all. How this love for her had stolen upon him and established itself so solidly while he was for the most part unaware, he could not explain to himself: a small, unassuming young woman who, though not plain, was certainly no diamond of the first water, who made no attempt to flirt or to attach him in any way. There were, however, those incredible blue eyes, the sweetness and serenity of her manner with its hints of humor, the flash of pretty, perfect teeth when she smiled. All these qualities had gradually become more attractive to him than all the charms of the accredited beauties of London. All his flirtations in the past had been games. At no time had his heart been engaged. He had never experienced that possessive feeling he had felt for Ursula after the first few days when he had regained consciousness.

Remembering now her enchantingly pretty arms with their round, dimpled elbows, and the lovely curve where her neck joined her shoulders, where he had longed to press his lips, he groaned aloud in his unhappiness, causing his sister much distress. She longed to comfort him, but did not dare to do so, for she knew he would hate her to even try and, after all, what comfort had she to offer him?

17

After all the excitement and dread of those first days after Ursula's arrival, then the lifting of spirits at Lord Henry's recovery, followed by the arrival of his sister and the ensuing social diversions, their sudden departure caused a distinct flattening of the atmosphere at Swan Court.

Ursula made every effort to ignore her depression and maintain her usual air of calm good nature. Her one breakdown before India she hoped India would ascribe to worry that Lord Henry might have suffered a more serious injury than had been thought. She expressed her worry aloud whenever the subject arose, but never initiated such a conversation. India respected her reticence and never questioned her about her feelings. She thought she knew them well enough, and if Ursula had the need to discuss them, she would turn to her bosom bow, for indeed, who else was there for her to turn to?

Ursula continued to ride out with the Rochdales and Blanche on every fine day. The burden of Sir Tarquin's love was not lightened by his soulful, pleading looks at her from time to time. He had few opportunities for private words with her, however, for Blanche, having lost in her bid to win Lord Henry, fell back with great determination upon Sir Tarquin, and clung to his side, monopolizing his attention.

After a week, even this came to an end when Sir Tarquin announced that he and his sisters would be leaving the next day for a long-planned visit to his aunt in Bath and would be away for at least two months.

Whether he could not face further meetings with his beloved while his heart was so sore from her rejection of his suit, or whether Blanche's desperation finally broke through her charm and frightened him into flight, no one knew. No doubt it was a combination of both. For though he had no feelings for Blanche as yet, his heart being entirely given to Ursula, he was not unaware that Blanche's flirting and flattery could come to assuage his bruised feelings and get him into a predicament where he might feel called upon in honor to make her an offer. Since he had no wish to marry Blanche, and no heart to be with Ursula, he fled.

Blanche, as close to despair as she had ever allowed herself to come, wrote to her friend old Lady Benbow, proposing herself for a visit. A reply came within the week, and Blanche, her bags packed in readiness, set off at once, despite the lamentations of the dowager. Even she, however, understood that Blanche must go where there were matrimonial prospects and would never have stayed so long at Swan Court had she not found two eligible gentlemen at hand.

The day Blanche left, India received this letter from Lady Elizabeth:

My dear Lady Swanson,

I write to tell you that we are assured by the doctor that Henry has suffered no lasting injury. I hope you have not been experiencing too much anxiety on Henry's behalf. Indeed, he is feeling very much better physically, though his spirits have been sadly depressed. London is very gay now and I have been rushed off my feet with visiting and parties, and of course shopping. When one as a rule gets to London but once a year, one must take every chance-sent opportunity to visit the shops, especially for the sake of the bairns, who grow so fast.

Do please give my regards to Lady Ursula and, if it

is appropriate by now, my felicitations. Your mother told me the day before we left that you were all in hourly expectation of an offer from Sir Tarquin, which would certainly be accepted. I am sure they have my sincerest best wishes for happiness if it is so.

Again allow me to thank you with all my heart for your goodness to us. My regards to your mother and Miss Vernon, and very best wishes to your dear husband. I hope you will find the time to respond to me as soon as may be convenient, for I must admit to an unbecoming curiosity about dear Lady Ursula, for I had entertained many hopes regarding her. I hope I do not distress you by alluding to them.

In the meantime, I remain, forever in your debt and hopefully ever your friend,

Elizabeth McFarland

India, at the breakfast table, read this through a second time before its full import reached her. "Oh, my God!" she cried, then burst into tears.

The dowager dropped her fork and Robert leapt to his feet to come rushing around the table to her. Ursula had not come down to breakfast. "My darling! What is it? Tell me at once!" Robert demanded, pulling her to her feet and into his arms.

"T-t-take me upstairs, please, Robert," she whispered.

Robert immediately led her away and up to their bedroom, she trying to choke back her sobs. "Now, what has happened, dearest girl?" Robert asked, as he pressed her down upon her chaise longue and seated himself beside her.

"Oh, Robert, read this—it will tell you everything."

Robert took Lady Elizabeth's letter and read it through. He frowned slightly. "Well . . . but I'm afraid I do not quite understand what about this has upset you so."

"Don't you see, darling? Your mother told Lady Elizabeth the day before they left that we were waiting for an offer to Ursula from Sir Tarquin and that she would accept him.

That same night he called her to his room because of a 'headache' and they left the very next morning.''

''But . . . but . . .''

''And he is still sadly depressed, though better physically and she is anxious to hear if an engagement has come about . . . and had entertained many hopes . . . Oh, it is all so clear. Your mother has ruined Ursula's chance for happiness and perhaps Lord Henry's as well with her meddling. I never mind when she pesters Cook, trying to change my menus, or ruins my flower arrangements, but to speak as an authority on matters that are no concern of hers is beyond anything!''

''What is all this about menus and flowers?''

''Oh, Robert, darling, forgive me for even speaking of such petty things. They do not matter.''

''Petty things can be very wearing to the mind, like drops of water on a stone. I would not have my mother interfering in your household.''

''Never mind that, Robert. It is Ursula that matters. Oh, how could she have told Lady Elizabeth such a thing? How could she? Poor darling Ursula.''

''Do you think she cared for him very much?''

''I am as sure of it as my feeling for you!''

''Ah, you angel,'' he said, kissing her warmly. ''And I suppose you can also tell me of his feelings,'' he added teasingly.

''Even you must have noticed his growing partiality for her.''

''Well, I am not so sensitive in these matters as you, but I admit I had begun to wonder. And then that day we walked to Cray's farm he asked me her brother's direction.''

''And you never told me?''

''I confess I forgot the matter entirely.''

''But what shall we do?''

''I know what I will do,'' he said grimly. ''As for you, you lie here for a while to compose yourself and then set about writing a letter to Lady Elizabeth to set the matter straight about Ursula." He kissed her again and then rose and crossed to the door. "I suppose it is not possible Sir Tarquin did make her an offer? He seemed smitten enough to me."

"If he did, his offer was refused, for he has gone away, and I know Ursula would never have accepted him."

"Very well. I know you are to be trusted in all matters of the heart," he said, smiling, and was gone.

He went back to the breakfast room, where his mother was just finishing her usual hearty breakfast.

"Well, my dear, is India all right now?"

"I hope that she is. If you are finished with your breakfast, I would like you to come into my study so that we may have a talk."

"Certainly, my son," she replied, and rose to precede him out of the room with stately dignity. No doubt, she thought happily, he needs to consult me about India's upset. I will assure him that young women are sometimes given to these starts when they are in her condition and that it is nothing to worry himself about.

When he had seated her in his study, he began at once, as was his way. "May I ask on what authority you told Lady Elizabeth that we were expecting an offer to Ursula from Sir Tarquin?"

"Authority? What can you mean? I did not feel any authority was required when I was but expressing my opinion," she said, bristling.

"According to her own words, you stated positively that *we* were all in hourly expectation and were sure she would accept him."

"I was expressing my opinion of the matter," she maintained stubbornly.

"Had either Ursula or Sir Tarquin confided to you any feelings of expectations, or had you heard from India or me such a thing?"

"There was no need. I could see he was head over

ears, and she could not expect to receive a better offer.''

"How can you possibly know that?''

"Why, only look at her, my son. A little dab of a creature with no beauty to speak of, no money, no experience in how to handle a gentleman,'' the dowager sniffed dismissively.

"Unlike Blanche, I suppose?'' he said sarcastically.

"Exactly! Blanche is wide-awake upon every suit, beautiful, witty, and—''

"Unmarried,'' Robert interrupted bluntly. "I did not notice, despite all her casting of lures, that either Sir Tarquin or Lord Henry made her an object of his attention. But never mind that,'' he said hastily as he saw her open her mouth to protest, "please go up now and put on your pelisse and bonnet. The carriage will be at the door in fifteen minutes.''

"But . . . but where are we going?''

"We are going,'' he said with great firmness, "to inspect the Dower House.''

"I do not care to see the Dower House.''

"You must have your own house to be mistress of. This house has a mistress, and I am assuming you do not want to return to Bath?''

The dowager glared at him for a long moment, but he met her gaze steadily, a steely look in his eyes. At last, when he did not relent, she tossed her head and left the room.

India had wasted no time in beginning her letter to Lady Elizabeth, and after the usual greetings wrote:

. . . and I cannot imagine why my mother-in-law would tell you such a tale about Ursula and Sir Tarquin, except that perhaps she had decided in her own mind that they would suit. Of course, it was clear that he was in love with her, but I can assure you that her affections were never engaged. Indeed, I believe it possible that he may have proposed and been refused, for he looked very glum for those days before he went off to Bath so suddenly to visit his aunt. I cannot be certain of this, of course, since Ursula has not confided it to me, but that is what I think happened. So you see, we are a much-depleted party here, since Blanche left this morning to visit her friend Lady Benbow. I fear it is very dull for dear Ursula after all the pleasant company we have had, and her spirits are much depressed.

My best respects to dear Lord Henry. Please tell him how happy we all are to hear that he is better, and how much we would welcome him for another visit whenever he chooses to come. Naturally, the same invitation includes you, though I am sure you deserve your town pleasures.

I hope to hear from you soon, and remain, dear Lady Elizabeth, ever your friend,

India Youngreaves

She ran downstairs to have her letter franked by her husband, passing her mother-in-law on the way up.

"Goodness, she looks thunderous—whatever did you say to her, Robert?"

"She is complying, against her wishes, with my request that she put on her bonnet and come for a drive with me," Robert said.

"A drive?"

"Yes, we are going to inspect the Dower House."

"Oh, Robert," India breathed, looking up at him with awe. "However did you persuade her?"

"I didn't try to persuade her. I simply told her. Something I should have done ages ago."

He handed her back her franked letter and she placed it on the hall table with other letters, then, throwing her husband a kiss, hurried away to the back of the house to avoid another encounter with the dowager. When she heard the carriage going down the drive, she went up and tapped at

Ursula's door, and was bidden to enter. Ursula looked up from her desk with a bright smile.

"I hope I am not interrupting you? I know you said you were not ill, but I just wanted to make sure for myself," India said, crossing the room to kiss her friend's cheek.

"I am very well. It was just that I could not seem to fall asleep for so long last night that I decided to be lazy this morning."

India thought her friend looked distinctly pale, and her eyes were dull, despite the bright smile. "I had a letter from Lady Elizabeth this morning."

"Oh! What did she say?" A spot of color appeared in Ursula's cheeks.

"Only that the doctor says all is well with Lord Henry and that she is very busy seeing friends and shopping. I . . . er . . . gave the letter to Robert, who must have gone off with it," India said, crossing her fingers behind her back, "or else you could read it for yourself. She sent her fond regards to you. I have already sent her a reply, which will be going out shortly. I feel sure we shall hear from her again quite soon."

"Yes, no doubt," Ursula said, her body seeming to droop and the color fading from her cheeks. India wished she could think of some punishment fit for her mother-in-law, who had brought all this unhappiness about with her meddling. Then she thought, brightening, that Robert had probably already accomplished this, for nothing anyone could do could be worse punishment for the dowager than being forced to leave Swan Court.

"And I am sure that now he has been assured by the London doctor that all is well, he will return to finish his visit with us," India continued brightly. When her friend did not respond to this, she went on determinedly, "And I will be extremely glad to have him, for I do so like having visitors and company—I wonder why Sir Tarquin went away so suddenly?"

"That, I fear, must be laid at my door, dearest. He . . . he proposed to me and I refused him, and the daily meetings became too uncomfortable for him after that. I am sorry to have deprived you of even your neighbor's visits, India."

"What nonsense! As though you need blame yourself for refusing a man's proposal. I am glad you did, for he was not really right for you, in my opinion. What a goose you are, darling, to talk so."

"Oh, India, you are so kind to me, and all I repay you with is my foolishness. I wonder you can bear me anymore."

"You, foolish? Never!"

"Oh, yes, very foolish, for I allowed myself to develop an unsuitable attachment and now I am so unhappy and such a burden to you—now when you should have no cares put upon you."

"An unsuitable attachment—for Lord Henry?" Ursula only nodded, fearing to cry if she spoke. "But, darling girl, what is unsuitable about that? It is the most suitable match I could imagine for you!"

"No, it was idiotic of me—I knew that he could not . . . but then he said things that seemed to show . . . I allowed myself to think he . . . But I was wrong."

"I don't think you were wrong. I could not help noticing the way he looked at you. I cannot believe for one minute that I am wrong about this. He will come back. You will see!"

18

Despite her efforts to maintain a cheery facade before her friends, Ursula's spirits were sadly lowered. She had done that which she promised herself she would not do—let her affections become engaged where she knew only unhappiness for herself could ensue. Or rather, she amended her thoughts, she could not actually accuse herself of actively encouraging her feelings to grow, for it had been quite the reverse once she had realized what was happening. However, it had been too late when she became aware of her danger, and though she had taken herself severely to task, her heart had continued on its way without consultation. She had realized the extent of the damage already done when India had told her of Lord Henry's headache. She had felt quite faint for some moments and her heart had its say undeterred, crying out silently, "Oh, my love, my dearest love," over and over so that she barely registered anything else India was saying. In her despair that he had suffered more serious injury than they thought, with God only knew what horrible results—madness, or even death!—she had lost control and sought the comfort India could give her. She knew then that her peace had disappeared forever. She had fallen in love with a man who could never love her in return.

Having once admitted this to herself as she sobbed on India's shoulder, she also decided not to speak of her feelings to her friend, since to do so would only cause India unhappiness, as well as confirm their reality to herself. She was not trying to hide from the truth, but she was not willing to dwell upon it either, knowing that to do so would only keep the pain alive. However, her old habit of confiding in India had at last overcome her resolve.

A few days after India's letter to her, Lady Elizabeth wrote again, this time to Ursula, proposing that she come to London for a visit: " . . . for two weeks only, my dear, before I return to my family. I am alone here now and would so enjoy someone to go about with." She had a great deal more to say in urging this project, but those two sentences at last allowed Ursula to be persuaded by India to go. If Lady Elizabeth were alone, that meant Lord Henry had left London. There would be no chance then of further damage to her heart by his proximity. By the end of the day it had been settled and a letter of acceptance sent off to Lady Elizabeth. The following day was spent in packing, and on the next day she was to set forth, with Carey, in Robert's best traveling carriage. He had insisted upon this, saying he had no need of it himself, since he had no intention of traveling anywhere. He also insisted on providing two postilions to ride with the coach for protection.

As she came down to breakfast dressed for travel, she heard India saying indignantly, " . . . she is not chasing after Lord Henry to London, Mother! He is not *in* London. Lady Elizabeth invited her especially to keep her company because she is alone there now."

There was an audible disbelieving sniff from the dowager, and it was all Ursula could do to stop herself from returning to her room and unpacking her cases. She was, however, almost to the door of the breakfast room, with Crigly waiting to enter after her with a covered dish, and to turn and flee upstairs would make it apparant to all that she had overheard. She could not allow India to be upset by such knowledge, so she resolutely said a loud, cheery "Good morning" to Crigly and passed on into the breakfast room. Her high color was ascribed by India and Robert to her excitement over traveling, and they were much gratified to see it.

As she was bowled along in the carriage, Ursula's anger at the dowager's spitefulness gradually cooled. The old lady was only bitter that Lord Henry had eluded the wiles of her niece, Blanche, for surely she could not really believe that she, Ursula Liddiard, would pursue any gentleman.

Her heart gave a little jolt at even the thought of meeting him again—but of course he would not be there. Would he? No, certainly not, or Lady Elizabeth would not have written that she was alone. Then, being only human, Ursula could not help the thought from forming before she could stop it, that perhaps Lady Elizabeth would write and tell him of her guest. Would he then come back to London? No, of course he would not! If he had wanted more of my company, she reminded herself grimly, he need not have left Swan Court. She had this scalding thought for company on her trip to London, and a very dreary trip it seemed.

Her welcome, however, was all that she could have wished, and assuaged her sore heart. Lady Elizabeth was all smiles and warm embraces and bubbling plans for every moment of their two weeks together.

"Darling Ursula," she cried, "I am so glad to see you! You will not mind if I call you so, will you? And you must call me Elizabeth from this moment. It is lovely to have company! I cannot do with being alone, but must always have someone dear by me, and since that wretch Henry went off to the Alvanleys'—he said he could bear London no longer—I have become quite forlorn. Now, my love, you are not to claim exhaustion, for you are too young and healthy to do so, but I will take you up to wash and change and then we are going to Madame Celine's, where I have had some new gowns made up, then I must call on my old aunt, for I promised to bring you around at once—she quite dotes on Henry, you see—and tonight we dine with the Flytes, old

friends of mine who are eager to meet you and made this
dinner party especially for that purpose.''

This stream of ebullient chatter covered Ursula's initial
shyness, as it was meant to do, and carried them up the stairs
to a very comfortable bedroom prepared for Ursula's use.
Carey was waiting, and as Ursula's cases were carried in,
she hurriedly began unpacking to find a walking dress for
her mistress's excursion onto the streets of London. Lady
Elizabeth left her to wash and change, and in thirty minutes
Ursula emerged in a figured dimity and fetching bonnet and
they set off at once for Madame Celine's. There, not only
had Lady Elizabeth three new gowns to be tried on for final
fitting, but there was also a gown of white spider gauze for
Ursula. Lady Elizabeth must have given a very exact descrip-
tion of Ursula's figure, for it needed only a few minor
adjustments.

Ursula protested with great embarrassment at accepting
this gift, but Lady Elizabeth only smiled and brushed all
objections aside, saying, ''Surely you can indulge me in this,
dear Ursula, when it gives me so much pleasure.''

There was not much Ursula could say to this, so she
thanked Lady Elizabeth graciously and accepted it. After this
they went to call upon Mrs. Charlbury, Elizabeth's aunt. She
was very old and very tiny, her face a mask of wrinkles from
which sparkled a pair of very bright black eyes. She surveyed
Ursula from head to foot and nodded approvingly.

''You'll do, my girl. I like to see a young woman with
flesh on her bones. Means good health. Good breeder, too.''

Ursula was startled and blushed and didn't know where
to look. Elizabeth laughed and took over the conversation
for a time to divert the old lady's thoughts. Mrs. Charlbury
could not be diverted for long, however, and returned to her
object. Clearly it was firmly established in her mind that this
young woman who had rescued her favorite nephew from
death was to be the future Lady Somerton. She had heard
Elizabeth's favorable report on the girl and gathered from

her that she was harboring some hopes for such a union, and decided at once upon seeing the girl that Henry must have her.

"Where is Henry?" Mrs. Charlbury demanded.

"He is making a visit to the Alvanleys," Elizabeth replied. "You were great friends with the dowager Lady Alvanley, were you not, Aunt?"

"He should be here to attend this girl who saved his life," the old lady declared firmly, ignoring Elizabeth's question.

"I only invited Lady Ursula after he deserted me for the Alvanleys, Aunt. I felt the need of company, you see. It is so much more amusing to have someone to go about with and gossip with about the people we meet at parties and—"

"Great heaven, what a rattle you have become, Elizabeth, your tongue seems loose on both ends. I am tired now. Send Henry to me as soon as he returns. Lady Ursula, I like you. You will do very well. Good day to you both."

They were dismissed, and left accordingly, both grateful to be out of range of the old lady's forthright tongue. Ursula sat in the carriage quite tongue-tied with embarrassment, while Elizabeth simply could not think of a way to explain her aunt's eccentric behavior without further upset to her guest, and finally decided it was best not to attempt an explanation at all.

The Flytes' dinner party that evening was a lovely, even soothing experience. The young Flytes were beautifully mannered and much too well-bred to exhibit vulgar curiosity. There was only one reference to Ursula's adventure when, upon introduction, Mrs. Flyte said, "Ah, how charming to meet a real heroine." This could have been an oppressive remark had she not followed it immediately by a compliment upon Ursula's gown—the blue violet with silver ribbons that was Ursula's favorite.

There were some twenty other guests, who, though eager to meet her, did not stare at her or ask questions. They were mostly young people and eager to enjoy themselves. After an excellent dinner there was impromptu dancing, and though Ursula did not dance, she found there was always a young man seated beside her making lighthearted conversation. She marveled at the kindness of her hostess, who had clearly heard all there was to know about this particular guest and had invited the company accordingly to make a lively, pleasant evening for her.

There were many other charming parties in the following two weeks, and it became clear to Ursula that Elizabeth had dined out frequently on the story of her brother's accident and rescue before Ursula had arrived. Perhaps that was why Lord Henry had left London. Unable any longer to face questions and teasing, he had fled London in exasperation. Or had he only gone when he learned that she had been invited? And, no, none of that, she chided herself. These idle speculations were pointless. She had promised herself that she would not indulge in any fantasies concerning Lord Henry. She would not avoid any discussion of him if it arose, and would attempt to respond naturally and interestedly, but without any intensity. Never for one moment would she betray her feelings with melancholy sighs or abstracted silences, nor, especially, any eager response at the sound of the door knocker. Nor did she do so. Even Lady Elizabeth wondered if it were possible the girl had no interest in Henry after all.

In fact, if anyone sighed or was silent or looked up eagerly at the sound of the door knocker, it was Elizabeth herself. For she had written Henry at once when she received Ursula's acceptance to come for a visit. He had left London to escape the constant barrage of questions about his accident, in some irritation with his sister for spreading the story about town. He had been on his way to the Alvanleys', where he knew he would be welcome, but had changed his mind and gone instead to his friend Poynton, feeling that the lively Alvanley household did not suit his mood.

Elizabeth's letter, therefore, was returned to her. Much

vexed, she pondered upon where he could have taken himself. At last, on a chance, she redirected it in care of Poynton at Brook House. By the time it reached there, Ursula was beginning her second week in London. However, Henry, too restless for fishing and finding the quiet and peace he sought only breeding grounds for unhappy thoughts, had decided that the lively Alvanleys would better suit his mood after all, and he moved on. Poynton returned Elizabeth's letter with this news, though not with any information as to his whereabouts, for Henry had not said where he was going and Poynton had surmised he was returning to London to spend the last days of his sister's visit with her before she returned to Scotland. Frustrated and at a complete stand, Elizabeth tore the letter into pieces and flung them into the fire. She could do no more. If he wanted to ruin all his chances with the girl by stravaging about the countryside just when he could fix his interests with her most firmly, it was upon his own head.

19

Life at Swan Court, though sadly reduced in company, was not without some excitement for those still there. For two days while Robert patiently conducted his mama over every inch of the Dower House, she had maintained a stony, disdainful silence. On the third day he began to lose patience.

"Since you find nothing to improve, Mama, I take it there can be no objection to setting the day for your removal here at once."

The dowager's closely held-in anger burst forth. "You expect me to move into this wretched place where the carpets are faded, the draperies moth-eaten, and the paint peeling off the walls?"

"Certainly not, Mama. I think you had best call in the decorators at once," he responded blandly.

Thereafter, though the dowager's indignation still smoldered, it was banked down considerably under an air of martyrdom. Gradually, however, as she became more immersed as the days passed in the ordering of new furniture, draperies, and carpets, as well as a new dinner service, and in interviewing prospective servants and ordering about the gardener, even this vanished under the gloriously fulfilling role of being mistress of a household once again with no one to say her nay.

She wrote excitedly to Blanche, imploring her to come back and help her make decisions about colors and patterns, but Blanche responded that such things bored her to fits and she would come for a short visit just to see it when everything was in order.

India wrote of all these events to Ursula in reply to Ursula's letter telling her of all her experiences in London. She mentioned only by the way that Lord Henry was visiting his friends the Alvanleys, but had no comment to make on the fact. India was devastated to learn that Henry had not reappeared on the scene once Ursula had arrived, for she was in no doubt at all that Lady Elizabeth had written to her brother at once to inform him of the impending visit, as well as that the rumor about Ursula and Sir Tarquin was a false one and that, in fact, Sir Tarquin was in Bath on a long visit. Still, she thought, there was another week to be passed in London, and surely before it ended he would have his sister's letter and return.

The days of that last week passed by in London, however, with no reappearance of Henry, and despite all her efforts not to be borne down by unhappiness, Ursula's heart grew heavier with each swiftly passing day. She went about unflaggingly with Elizabeth, shopping, visiting, dining out, driving and riding in the park. She still smiled and looked serene, but to her eyes everything seemed to be shrouded in an enveloping gray veil.

Elizabeth was convinced the girl was still heart whole and had no more feelings for Henry than, according to India Youngreaves, she had for Sir Tarquin Rochdale. Elizabeth thought this at least until the last evening, when, coming quietly into the drawing room, she saw Ursula sitting in a window seat in the last rays of the sun, which glistened on a tear trailing down her cheek. Ursula was the very picture of misery, and Elizabeth's heart was wrung with pity for her. Very quietly she backed out of the room, to reenter noisily ten minutes later. She was greeted with a smile, though the smile did not, Elizabeth noticed, reach her eyes.

Early the next morning Ursula set off for Swan Court. The two ladies embraced warmly and shed some tears to be parting, but it was, in truth, a relief for both of them. Elizabeth was dreadfully homesick and longing for her husband and children, and Ursula felt she could bear her sadness better away from London and the apparently unquenchable hope that she might see Lord Henry. She knew it could not be a good thing for her to be in his company anymore, but she felt that even one brief look at his face would afford some warming to the cold feeling around her heart.

No brief glimpse was allowed to her; however, she found some easement in the tears she allowed herself in the carriage, with only Carey to see them. When they had run their course, she dried her eyes and explained to the abigail that she was sorry to be leaving dear Lady Elizabeth since there could be no guarantee that she would ever see her again, as she lived so far away. Carey, who thought she knew very well what her mistress was crying about, as well she did, made sympathetic noises and kept her own counsel.

Ursula arrived back at Swan Court at ten of that same evening and found both Robert and India waiting to welcome her home. The warmth of their greetings made her feel it was a real homecoming, and she was much solaced. After she had removed her bonnet and pelisse, they led her into the dining room, where a supper had been laid out for her. Her dragging spirits had curbed her appetite all day, but now with these good friends she found she could laugh and talk and eat hungrily.

They lingered over the meal for over an hour while Ursula told them all the things she had done and all the people she had met in London, some of whom had remembered her from her Season five years previously, and most of whom remembered India and Robert and sent their regards to them.

Then they told her of all that had been happening while she was away, mostly to do with the dowager and the Dower House.

"Has she already removed there?"

"Oh, dear, no, the renovations she has demanded won't be finished for at least another week," India said.

"So long for a bit of painting and new draperies?"

"Ho! A bit of paint and draperies!" Robert said. "You can't know my mama at all if you think she would give up Swan Court for only a bit of paint. No, no, she comes somewhat dearer than that, I fear. Or perhaps I should say she goes dearer than that."

"You will be truly amazed, dearest, when you see it," India said. "Every drapery and curtain in the place has come down to be replaced, every carpet raised and discarded, new furnishings throughout. Two bedrooms are finished, one each for Mother and Blanche. I think Blanche is advising her, for they are in almost daily communication now, though Blanche won't come to help her because there is a gentleman staying with Lady Benbow, and Blanche has hopes. But the furniture is all the latest rage, crocodile crouches and Egyptian motifs everywhere—quite hideous, actually."

She paused for breath and Ursula exclaimed, "But it must be costing the earth!"

"Oh, she does not trouble herself about that, since the bills are all sent to me," Robert replied quite cheerfully.

"But . . . how dreadful!"

"No, no," Robert said, "well worth every penny. Think of the peace we shall have. Indeed, that we already have, for she rises early, has her breakfast, and orders the carriage, with a basket of food already put up by Cook and stowed upon the seat in case hunger overtakes her during the day, and only returns for her dinner and an early bed. I would not want to be one of those poor workmen there, for I am sure she makes their lives miserable. On the other hand, it gets things done faster if she is there to oversee them, and she will soon be able to move in permanently, much to the relief of all. My mother has never been a person I would choose to live with, given the choice," he added candidly.

Ursula went to her bed so warmed and cheered by her

friends' kindness that she fell asleep almost at once and slept soundly the night through.

In the morning her heart was lighter than it had been for weeks, and she congratulated herself that she was evidently not doomed to unhappiness forever just because she had been blighted in love.

Over breakfast India proposed a drive to the Dower House so that Ursula could see for herself all that was going forward there. Ursula agreed, and Robert had a light open carriage brought around with two of this steadiest horses between the shafts. He fussed about settling India comfortably with cushions and rugs and many instructions to the coachman to drive with extreme care. India was in her sixth month now and he could hardly bear to let her out of his sight.

The Dower House, when they came to it, proved to be a gem of Tudor design, set in beautifully kept gardens, now in riotous blossom. Ursula gasped with pleasure.

"Yes, it is a treasure of a house, is it not? However, I am very much afraid the inside fights with the lovely exterior and does not come out the victor. Shall we go in?"

They stepped down from the carriage and entered through the open front door into a chaos of ladders and trestles and workmen, in the midst of which stood the dowager, issuing orders and counterorders and generally confusing everyone in the process. The great hall was paneled in dark oak, and in the far wall was an enormous fireplace large enough to roast a whole ox. The dowager hadn't seen them yet, so India took Ursula's arm and led her down the hall, past the beautiful staircase, into the dining room, which was also paneled in oak on three walls. On the fourth wall was a covering of old gilded leather. The ceilings were embossed with Tudor roses and crowns, and the doors and windows were canopied.

"What a lovely old room," Ursula exclaimed. "When was it built?"

"According to the date carved into the mantelpiece in the

great hall—1578. I am glad you are seeing it before it is all changed and 'brought up-to-date,' as my mother-in-law says. The only finished rooms are two of the bedrooms—and I believe the kitchen is nearly finished.''

"What do you think she is going to do down here?''

"Only paint and new furnishings, I believe.''

"Now, in here I think—'' the dowager said as she entered the dining room with a man in tow. "Why, India, my dear, I did not know you were here. Do you think it quite wise of you, dearest, to go about in the carriage now? I really must speak to Robert . . . And Lady Ursula! So you are back. You look fagged to death, my dear. I fear your trip cannot have been successful.''

"Good morning, Lady Swanson. It was a very busy two weeks. How very busy you have been yourself.''

"Ah, well, if you do not watch over them every moment, they will never do it as you want it. And since I am forced to make a new home for myself in my old age, I feel I want it to be just what will give me most comfort in my few remaining years,'' the dowager replied with a heavy sigh.

"How fortunate you are to have such a beautiful home. It is well worth all your hard work and I'm sure you will enjoy it all the more for knowing you created it all yourself.''

"Oh, I have never been known to shun hard work. You must go up and see the bedrooms that are finished. One is mine and the other is Blanche's room.''

"Oh, is she coming or a visit?''

"I wish she would, but she will come as soon as she can. She is still with Lady Benbow and there is a young man visiting who will not hear of her leaving. It was love at first sight, for him at least. He is a Mr. Martingale, from *the* Martingales, you know, a regular Croesus. She could not do better if she searched the earth, but she is so very particular, the dear girl.'' India and Ursula exchanged a swift but carefully blank glance. "So, Lady Ursula, you did not find Lord Henry in London?''

"No, indeed I did not, Lady Swanson, nor did I expect to do so. It was because he was not there that Lady Elizabeth had a need for my company," Ursula replied evenly.

"Pho, pho, pho, my girl. I am sure he could have arranged to return if he had so desired. But you will remember I told you to beware of these young gentlemen who start flirtations to pass the time if they lack other entertainment. I did warn you."

"Come, Ursula darling, we must be on our way if we are to make our call on Lady Rochdale," India interposed, taking her friend's arm.

"Call on Lady Rochdale? Why? Is Sir Tarquin back from Bath?" the dowager demanded.

"I believe it will be some weeks before he is expected," India replied. "We shall see you at dinner, Mother."

As they drove away, India pondered the problem of whether she should confess to Ursula the dowager's disastrous communication to Lady Elizabeth that she was confident had caused Lord Henry to leave so abruptly. She felt guilty at withholding this information from her friend, but what if it should give rise to a hope that might never be fulfilled? On the other hand, she felt in her heart that Lady Elizabeth would tell her brother the truth. Then surely he would declare himself, knowing that Ursula's heart and hand were still free. Oh, surely, surely he would!

20

Three days later, Blanche suddenly appeared among them without sending ahead any notice of her arrival.

"Since Aunt was always begging me to come at once to help her with her decorating, I did not think it necessary to write. Dear Lady Benbow was called away suddenly to a dying uncle's bedside, and I could hardly stay on there alone, though she begged me to stay just as long as I liked."

"But, Blanche, dearest, what of Mr. Martingale?" her aunt asked anxiously, as usual blurting out the very words Blanche wanted least to be heard.

"Mr. . . . ? Oh . . . Mr. Martingale. Goodness, Aunt, how should I know anything about him? He was there only a week and left at least three days ago. A most disagreeable man! I was happy to see the back of him, and had nearly succeeded in forgetting his existence entirely." She looked distinctly annoyed and her steely glance at her aunt held promise of a scold in store for the dowager.

India and Ursula exchanged a glance and looked away from each other hastily, for each saw laughter brimming in the other's eyes. Clearly Mr. Martingale had been too wily to be caught in Blanche's snares, and she was still smarting from his escape.

"Well, I am sure Mother will be very grateful for your help, Blanche," India said pacifically, "though, of course, I am sorry to hear of Lady Benbow's trouble. What uncle would that be, I wonder. There were several, as I remember.''

''I think she said his name was May . . . or something . . . an admiral,'' Blanche said. ''He lives in Northampton, very near the Alvanleys. Oh, speaking of them, I have heard a bit of news from that direction that might interest you all. Lord Henry is staying with the Alvanleys quite this age, and is held there, it seems, by the charms of a Miss Devere.'' She accompanied this *on-dit* with a spiteful smile.

''Devere? Now, I wonder what Devere that could be,'' India said lightly, not daring to look at Ursula, lest Blanche see it.

''Why, William Devere's daughter, of course. Just eighteen, and a great beauty. She only came out this season and cut quite a dash in London, they say,'' Blanche answered, her eyes avidly upon Ursula's face.

''I don't believe I have ever met any of the Deveres,'' Ursula said with a pretense of careless interest that was very difficult for her, since her mouth was suddenly dry and her lips almost too stiff to move. ''But then, I was in society so briefly and have been out of it so long I scarcely know anyone.''

''William Devere is the heir of old Septimus Devere,'' India said promptly, jumping in at once to gain time for her friend to recover and to frustrate Blanche further, ''whose mother was one of the Thorndykes. Simply swimming in money, what with their own and what the Thorndykes settled on their daughter, and connected to the best families in England. Refused to accept a title. Very proud, the Deveres, you know. They have always said Deveres did not need titles to distinguish them.''

''His brother, James, was an old beau of mine,'' the dowager said dreamily, ''a lovely dancing partner—but only a third son,'' she added, recovering her good sense abruptly.

By this time Ursula's partial paralysis was beginning to thaw and her backbone to stiffen. She turned to India with a smile. "Well, I hope he is not so smitten that he forgets to write to his sister. She had not a word from him while I was with her, and she worried so because of his injury. She quite dotes on her brother."

This brave speech earned her such a warmly approving look from India that Ursula winked at her. India resolved at once to write to Lady Elizabeth before the day was out to inform her of her brother's whereabouts.

Lady Elizabeth, however, had only that day received a letter from Henry, his first since he had left London. He had felt all this time that there was very little he had to say that he would be willing to put in writing. The outline of his story she knew well enough, and there was little she could do to help him, he thought.

It was true that he had lingered on at the Alvanleys' because of the arrival of Miss Devere. She was an enchanting child, only out one Season and already an accomplished flirt, secure in the knowledge that almost every man she met would seek her company and pay her compliments.

"I was such an unsightly tomboy, my mother quite despaired," she confessed naively to Henry, "but then I quite suddenly grew up and everything changed," she added with a tone of awe in her voice at her own fortune in growing up to be beautiful.

This, of course, charmed Henry, for there was so much innocence in it. Her flirtatious ways were a balm to his unhappiness, even though she treated every gentleman in the party in the same way. There was no vice in her, so few could resent her even-handed dispensation of her favors. She amused and distracted Henry, and that was enough to keep him there, not happily yet, for he still could not think of Ursula without a cloud of gloom settling over him, but at least with a sort of mindlessness he knew he could not find anyplace else right now.

It had now been nearly a month since he had seen Ursula, and yet when he allowed himself, he could see her face as clearly as though she stood before him. Each time he allowed this vision, he felt an actual physical pain in the region of his heart, so he supposed it was true that one could die of a broken heart if one indulged oneself in too much retrospection. He certainly did not want to die, so he rarely allowed himself to deliberately think of Ursula, though sometimes she slipped into his thoughts unbidden and caused him that wrenching pain. He supposed it would ease with time.

That was why he spent a great deal of time in Miss Devere's company, allowing himself to be diverted by her charming ways, almost willing himself to develop some feelings for her in order the more quickly to be rid of his unhappiness. Then he began to notice the girl's mama looking upon him speculatively, even indulgently, and drew back. He was aware that he was a matrimonial catch any mama would welcome, even despite the great disparity in the ages of Miss Devere and himself, for he was more than twelve years older than the girl. But did he want to be caught?

He wanted very much to be married, and to settle down in his own household, and raise his children. The problem was that this longing had overtaken him as he was falling in love with Ursula, and he could not now erase the image of her as mistress of that household and mother of those children. He knew it was only a month, and these violent emotions he still had with regard to her would take a great deal longer than a month to wane, but he still could not imagine anyone taking her place. Certainly not Miss Devere, enchanting little minx though she was.

No, he was in no danger of losing his heart to Miss Devere. She was quite lovely, to be sure, with the schoolgirl dew still fresh upon her despite her wildly successful first Season, but he felt no compulsion at all to make love to her, even were he to be allowed to do so. She was too volatile, too filled with a spoilt beauty's caprices to give him the peace it was almost too easy to imagine in the embrace of Ursula.

He almost groaned aloud at the thought that he had never held her in his arms, never kissed her.

Feeling as he did, he knew he must not allow himself to give rise to any hopes in Miss Devere's mama's breast that he was likely to make her daughter an offer. He didn't think any such hopes existed in Miss Devere, for the simple reason that she was, at the moment, much too happy being the belle of the ball wherever she went, and quite clearly intended to break as many hearts as possible before she settled down into marriage. Apart from this, she had never shown any decided partiality for him, for which he now saw he had every reason to be grateful.

However, that evening after dinner Miss Devere seemed willing to linger in his company, favoring him with a languishing glance from beneath her extravagant eyelashes. Perhaps her mama had been talking to her and she hoped for another proposal to add to her list. Later her mama tapped the seat beside her on a sofa with her fan in clear invitation to Lord Henry to sit beside her, and then spent quite twenty minutes expanding upon all her darling's talents and successes.

When his host nudged him that same evening and intimated that he smelled orange blossoms in the air each time he came near him, and lifted an eyebrow suggestively in Miss Devere's direction, Henry decided it was time for him to pay a visit to his friend Poynton.

In the meantime, he assured his host that while he found Miss Devere amusing, he had no romantic inclinations toward her. He also informed him that he would be leaving in a few days for his long-promised and overdue visit to Poynton. He spoke very casually, for he did not want to give the impression he was running from danger.

When he reached his room that night, he dashed off a note to Poynton asking if it would be convenient to come in a few days. He knew it was unnecessary to write, for Poynton was always there, rarely had any other company, and always welcomed him if he came and did not object when he left. He was a very self-sufficient man.

Henry also wrote, at last, to Elizabeth, telling her very little beyond the fact that he was going to Poynton's soon, and if she cared to write, she could send it here, and if he had left, they would send it on to him.

A very slow week then passed for Henry while he tried to make up his mind to go, always seeming to defer his departure for one more day. He contrived to be away from the house as much as possible, and often was out on long rides about the countryside. However, he could hardly avoid dinner and the socializing afterward, and became increasingly aware that whatever expectations Miss Devere might have, her mama had fixed upon him as the perfect mate for her flighty daughter. He avoided all private *tête-à-têtes* with the daughter, but Mrs. Devere was not to be so easily diverted. He presented a blandly courteous manner to all her blandishments and teasings and silently cursed his friend Poynton for being such a laggard in responding to his note, though he knew perfectly well he was welcome to come and go at Brook House as he pleased. It was simple inertia that held him where he was.

At last a letter came for him—but from Elizabeth, not Poynton. In it she scolded him roundly for disappearing without telling her where he was going, and of how she had written to him at the Alvanleys' and then to Poynton's with news she thought he would be glad to hear, and both times her letter had been returned.

She then proceeded to tell him her news. First, of her letter from India completely denying any engagement between Lady Ursula and Sir Tarquin, nor any thought of one, there being no partiality on Ursula's part in that direction. Then that Sir Tarquin had proposed to Lady Ursula, according to young Lady Swanson, and been refused, since he had gone off to Bath only a few days after they themselves had quitted Swan Court. She told him of Lady Ursula's visit of two weeks in London—here Henry groaned aloud and cursed most awfully—and went on at great length to him about how stupidly he had behaved in not writing to her and of missed opportunities. After news of the bairns' latest exploits and the health of darling Brian, she closed with the hope that, armed with her assurance that Ursula's heart was still to be won, he would set about winning it at once. From what she could assess of the situation, she said, Lady Ursula was very unhappy about something, that according to young Lady Swanson it had begun with their own abrupt departure, and she would leave him to make of that what he would.

He read this letter three times and then sat staring into space in a dazed sort of way for some time. At last he rang for his man and ordered his bags to be packed ready for a start immediately after breakfast the next day.

Be damned to Poynton's letter. If he could not sit down and write a response, he would have to suffer an uninvited visitor.

21

On the same day that Henry received his sister's letter, Ursula received one from the same source, for Lady Elizabeth believed in immediate action. She told Ursula that she had at last heard from her brother, who had been visiting with the Alvanleys for some weeks, but that now he had tired of it and was going on to his friend Poynton in a few days and from there she felt sure he would take the opportunity, being so nearby, to pay a visit.

Ursula, at the breakfast table, was not gladdened by this news, though she knew Lady Elizabeth meant her to feel encouraged. Ursula felt in her heart that all was lost. She was alone with India, for Robert had gone away on business for the day and the dowager and Blanche had breakfasted early and left for the Dower House. India looked up from her own letters to give her friend a bit of news from London, and saw Ursula's face set in a mask of misery. She rose at once and came around the table.

"Dearest girl, what is wrong?"

"Why, it . . . Nothing, India, I . . ."

"But of course there is. You would not look that way over nothing. Is it bad news?" Wordlessly Ursula held out Lady Elizabeth's letter for India to read. "But this is good news! Lord Henry to be in our neighborhood again! How delightful it will be to see him."

"I doubt he will come here."

"But why do you say that? After all, his sister tells us it

183

is so, and she would say that only if he had told it to her himself.''

"He may have said that only to put her off the scent."

"Off the scent—why, whatever can you mean, Ursula?"

"I think Blanche is right. He has been with the Alvanleys several weeks, and why would he stay so long if there were not some particular attraction? Miss Devere. I think Blanche had the right of it, after all. He has fallen in love at . . . at last."

She made this speech quietly, in an almost monotonous tone of voice, though her hands were clenched so tightly the knuckles shone white. With the words "at last," however, a sob broke through and she flung her arms upon the table and her head down upon them and cried as heartbrokenly as a child.

India bent over and hugged her heaving shoulders, kissed the top of her head again and again, and murmured comforting sounds. At last, when the sobs had abated somewhat, she whispered, "You are wrong, darling, I know it. Remember the time in London when you confessed to me that he was your beau ideal? Ever since then I have felt you were meant for each other, but sometimes Cupid mixes up things in his calendar and things go all awry for a time. It is my belief that though you were not aware of it, you have always loved him and he was meant to be yours at last—only circumstances got in the way. How else could one interpret your meeting again in such an unbelievable way— and his falling in love with you, for I know he did and that he will come soon to tell you so. I promise you."

"Oh, India, I kn-know you want to m-make me feel better, but d-don't make up stories for me as though I w-were a child. He would not have g-gone away so suddenly if he . . . and b-by then it was too late f-for me. I d-did not mean to f-fall in love, it was j-just there one day before I c-could stop it. It is very painful. I w-wish very much not to b-be in love."

At this confusion India could not restrain herself any longer. "It was Mother," she blurted out. "She told Lady Elizabeth that you were on the point of betrothal to Sir Tarquin and that you were going to accept him. They left that very next day, you remember. I know it was because of that. He could not bear it—to stay and see you become another's. If you could have seen his face that morning. Truly he looked in the most dreadful pain, and I had no trouble believing he was plagued by headache. It was only after I heard from Lady Elizabeth that I realized what had happened."

Ursula raised her swollen, tear-filled eyes during this speech and turned a stunned look upon India. "She told Elizabeth that I . . . that I . . . ? Why would she do such a thing?"

"Believe me, dearest, I do not think it was to make mischief or anything evil. She saw that he had fallen in love with you, and no doubt decided in her mind that it would be a good match for you, and for her the thing was settled. She says things like that to make herself important and to feel herself in charge of events. Since she has settled the matter to her own satisfaction, it must be so. Do you understand?"

"But it does make mischief, even if she does not do it for that reason," Ursula protested, applying her handkerchief to eyes and nose.

"Indeed it does, and when we found it out, Robert administered her a tremendous set-down. I was so upset, you see, and crying, which he cannot bear, and somehow while telling him of this thing, I also let slip some of the other little annoying things she does, and that is how she happens to be going to live at the Dower House at last."

"But why did you not tell me this before, India?"

"I thought that I might have been wrong and you did not care, for you have never said anything, and if I was right and you did, I feared to give you a false hope if I was wrong about his feelings. Now I know how you feel, and I feel more than ever that I was right about his feelings.''

"Yet, I fear it is still a false hope.''

"I do not think so,'' India replied stoutly, "and apart from all that, there is the fact that if he is so near, it would be the outside of good manners not to call, after all you did for him, and since he was a guest in this house.''

"I think I would rather he not come at all for those reasons. It is far better for me that I do not see him at all. Only, I cannot understand how, if it were so that he left for the reasons you said, he could have taken anyone's words as the truth about my feelings. I am sure I never gave anyone reason to believe I returned Sir Tarquin's love.''

"Well, you were very friendly to Sir Tarquin, and Lord Henry may well have misinterpreted things, and Mother's news only confirmed them.''

"I find I cannot believe that. He may have resented not being first in my regard, as he thought, for he is a man accustomed to come first with females.''

India laughed. "How can you say such things of him? Why, he had no arrogance at all of that kind.''

"He does not show it, of course, for he is no coxcomb, but after so many years of girlish languishings and pursuing mamas, he would be less than human if he did not feel it a little. Sir Tarquin was very . . . open in his feelings, and I did not repulse him because he was a good, kind man and my friend. At the same time, I gave him no encouragement to think my feelings had become anything stronger than friendship allows.''

"I told Lady Elizabeth I felt that was the truth of it.''

"Good God, India! How could you tell her such a thing?''

"Because I wanted her to pass that news on to her brother, and I was very sure it was true.''

"And it evidently made very little difference to him, one way or another,'' Ursula replied, biting her lip to hold back tears.

"You cannot know that—"

"He left London," Ursula said flatly.

"But that was before he knew you were coming. Lady Elizabeth said she was alone there, remember, and wanted company. She would not have said that if her brother were still with her," India said persuasively.

Ursula only shook her head and rose. "No more, India dearest. I cannot bear any more. I think I will ride now, if you will not mind my leaving you alone for a time?"

"Of course not. You are to do just as you like. But I must say just this—remember, I know in my heart that he loves you and I refuse to believe a man like Lord Henry is so volatile he could change his mind so quickly. It has been only a month, you know, since he left here."

"Has it been only a month?" Ursula replied drearily as she turned and trailed out of the room. When she had changed into her habit, she went to the stables and waited patiently for the mare to be saddled, then rode off, refusing to allow a groom to attend her, saying she did not mean to leave the park.

After a time she saw that she had come to the gates of the Dower House and stopped to take in once more the beauty of its facade. She turned after a moment to ride on, when she heard a carriage approaching, and was hailed by the passenger, Mr. Phillips-Glenn-Phillips.

"Dear Lady Ursula, how fortunate to meet you. It seems such an age. How do you do?"

"Very well, Mr. Phillips. And you?"

"In the pink, dear lady, in the pink of condition. Are you coming up?"

"Up?"

"To the house. Lady Swanson has been so kind as to allow me to give my opinion in decorating matters."

"Perhaps another day—"

"Oh, but you must, truly you must. Lady Swanson will

be devastated to learn you were at her very door and would not stop for a moment.''

Ursula seriously doubted that, but she cared so little what she did that she trotted her mare docilely alongside the carriage up the drive to the door.

The dowager must have been listening for the carriage, for she came out at once, all smiling welcome. She cast a surprised look at Ursula, but greeted her warmly, happy to have any audience for her labors.

''Welcome to you both! Mr. Phillips, you are just in time. So many tiresome decisions. Do come in. Dear Blanche is just through there in the dining room.''

Blanche turned as they entered, nodded to Ursula, and flashed an alluring smile at Mr. Phillips-Glenn-Phillips. Ursula was much surprised, for on previous occasions when she had been present, Blanche had all but ignored the gentleman. Ursula could not help but wonder if since he was the only male present she felt obliged to flirt with him. He was only too enchanted, and bowed over her hand to plant a courtly kiss upon her knuckles.

''Now, do give us your advice, Mr. Phillips. We were trying to think what might be best to do about this dreadful gloomy old paneling. I thought we might just have it taken out, but Blanche has suggested painting it white. What do you think?''

At her words, Ursula nearly gasped aloud with dismay, and Mr. Phillips-Glenn-Phillips visibly shuddered. He bravely smiled, however, and said, ''Oh, my dear Lady Swanson, please allow me to pray that you do neither.''

''But it makes the room so dark, you see,'' Blanche said with a little moue of distaste.

''Now, perhaps, Miss Vernon, but the room is made for evening entertainment, and when the wood is highly polished, it reflects the candlelight in so lovely a way. And your fair beauty would be indescribably bewitching framed against its dark glow.''

Blanche's lips turned up in a smugly gratified smile. "Well, I thank you, sir, and perhaps you are right and it should remain as it is. But this dreadful old leather hanging. Surely that could not prove a becoming setting for anyone."

"No, no, my dear. That will have to go, of course."

"I knew you would agree. Now, do come up and see all we have done abovestairs." She tucked her hand confidingly in his elbow and led him away.

Ursula hastily called a general good-bye and made her escape as the dowager went bustling off after the couple on the stairs.

With the help of a groom who had hurried out when the carriage had approached, she remounted and rode away. Once in the lane she let the horse have its way and they set off on a good gallop. While this went on, her mind was engrossed with her horse, but when at last she was forced to rein in for fear of overtiring the mare, her thoughts found their way at once into the same old channels, become deep ruts by now, and went on their usual course, round and round, finding no way out. For despite Lady Elizabeth's letter, and India's revelations, she could find no solace. She could not even be angry with the dowager when she was face-to-face with her so soon after learning what the woman had done. For had it been so catastrophic after all? Ursula knew, as well as she knew anything, that Elizabeth had written to her brother, if not to assure him that what the dowager had told her was untrue and he need no longer suffer a broken heart, then at least to pass along an item of news he would find of interest, since he was acquainted with all the parties. She would also tell him, naturally, of her visitor in London. That he had not made it his first object to hurry to Ursula's side to fix his interest spoke clearly of his lack of regard for her.

Having received his sister's communication, had he returned to London? Had he given any sign of interest since? Not another word from him since he had left—was that a sign of overpowering feelings for her? No, she could not think it!

When she came in from the stable, she tried to look cheerful for her friend's sake, for she felt much guilt for breaking down in that disgraceful way at the breakfast table and laying such a burden of sorrow on India's shoulders, when she should be doing everything possible to make this waiting time light and amusing for India.

"My dear, you will never guess," she said as she entered the drawing room, "our Blanche is starting a flirt with Mr. Phillips."

India gaped at her. "You surely cannot be serious."

"I assure you I am. I just happened to be passing when he came by on his way to the Dower House, summoned by the dowager to give his advice. Blanche took him in charge at once, casting smiles and melting looks. Oh, it was as good as a play."

India giggled and Ursula became infected, and soon they were in whoops. Robert came in and stood grinning at them.

"What unseemly behavior, I must say," he said.

"Oh, Robert, you will not believe it—do tell him, Ursula."

Ursula obliged in more detail, and he laughed delightedly until he heard of Blanche wanting to paint the oak paneling white in the dining room. Then his smile faded.

"I see I shall have to lay down a few laws to my mama abut how far she may go in her redecorating—and to Blanche as well. That I look forward to," he added with a gleam in his eye, for he enjoyed coming to daggers drawn with Blanche.

India sighed, her heart eased of some of its unhappiness for her friend, for it seemed to her that Ursula had come in from her ride in a more cheerful frame of mind. Perhaps she is coming to believe that what I have told her is true, India thought. "Tomorrow," she said, "we must drive over there. I simply have to find out if romance is truly flowering."

22

The carriage had been ordered, and by midmorning the next day the two friends were driven to the Dower House. The chaos of their first visit together had mostly disappeared, and the freshly painted and papered rooms stood ready to receive the furniture ordered for them. The drawing-room furnishings consisted so far of only two sofas set facing each other, one to either side of the fireplace, where a small fire burned cheerfully. The dowager and Blanche sat, one on each sofa, watching Mr. Phillips-Glenn-Phillips, who was overseeing three workmen in the hanging of draperies of rich blue velvet.

All this India and Ursula saw as the newly hired butler threw open the drawing-room door to announce their arrival. The dowager rose and surged forward.

"India, my dear child. Do come and sit down at once. Are you feeling quite well?"

"Very well, Mother, thank you."

"I really think you should not be racketing about in a carriage. I spoke to Robert, but of course no one ever listens to my advice, though I am sure I know more about it than either of you possibly could. In my day women knew better than to submit themselves to such dangers. Only think if there were an accident! Good morning, Lady Ursula."

"Good morning, Lady Swanson, Miss Vernon, Mr. Phillips," Ursula replied.

General geetings were exchanged and the ladies seated

themselves. Ursula complimented the dowager upon the color of the draperies.

"Yes, they have turned out very well, but then, I knew that color would do perfectly for this room," the dowager said complacently.

"Ah, dear Lady Ursula," Mr. Phillips-Glenn-Phillips cried, "you must give us your opinion upon the way we have hung them."

Before Ursula could respond, Blanche jumped to her feet and crossed the room to lay a hand possessively upon Mr. Phillips-Glenn-Phillips' arm. "Why, what is the problem, Valentine?" she cried. "They are just as we agreed they should be."

"Nothing at all, dear lady," he said soothingly as he patted her hand. "I was just angling for compliments."

"They look perfectly lovely, Mr. Phillips," Ursula said honestly. She and India exchanged a carefully stony glance.

"Thank you, Lady Ursula. I must compliment you upon your good taste," he said, laughing at his own joke. All the ladies dutifully followed suit.

"Oh, Mr. Phillips, how very droll you are. So amusing," Blanche cooed, looking up at him through her lashes.

"Ah, my dear, you are too kind," he said, staring into her eyes as though mesmerized.

"Not so. I am always the soul of truth. I cannot bear lies and flattery, but I do adore a man with a sense of humor."

India and Ursula did not dare look at one another. The workmen, having completed their job, made for the door, and the dowager rang for the butler. When he appeared, she ordered wine and biscuits for her guests.

"Why, Mother," India cried, "you are a long way along—a butler and supplies for entertaining already."

"Oh, yes, indeed," the dowager said proudly. "My cook has arrived and the butler is interviewing other help. Most of the furniture will have arrived by the end of the week. Oh, yes, we are well along."

After a time Ursula and India took their leave. Once in the carriage and through the gates, they looked at each other and began to laugh.

"Oh, dear," India cried, "you are right. Do you think she is seriously trying to attach him, or just practicing?"

"It is much too early to say for sure. Perhaps it is such an automatic response to an unmarried male that she cannot prevent herself. In any case, poor Mr. Phillips looks well and truly caught."

"Poor man," India said with another giggle. "Only think what a lovely couple they would make. And he is swimming in money, you know. Rich as Golden Ball."

"That will certainly make a great difference in Blanche's decision if she brings him up to scratch."

"Oh, Ursula, how naughty! What a deliciously vulgar expression."

When they arrived back at Swan Court they were met by Crigly with the news that a gentleman had arrived and awaited Lady Ursula in the drawing room. Ursule stopped dead, turned pale, and seemed to sway.

India took her arm in some alarm. "Who . . . who is it, Crigly?"

"Lord Herronly, m'lady."

Ursula sagged for an instant upon India's arm, then straightened herself and said with artificial brightness, "Good heavens, Rupert! What can he be doing here?"

They went into the drawing room still arm in arm. Lord Herronly rose. "Ursula, Lady Swanson, good day to you."

"Well, Rupert, this is a very great surprise. I hope nothing is wrong with your family," Ursula said, going forward, hands outstretched.

He took them and bent to kiss her cheek. "Dear girl. Yes, we are all well. But you look something pale and drawn."

"Nonsense, Rupert. I am in my usual bouncing good health. Now, sit down and tell me why you have come and why you are looking so grave."

"If Lady Swanson will not think me unforgivably rude, I think it would be best if we spoke privately."

India began to rise, but Ursula held her down. "Rupert, is this family business or has it to do only with me?"

"Er . . . well . . . actually, only to do with you, my dear."

"Then India must stay. We have no secrets between us," Ursula replied firmly.

"No, really, Ursula, perhaps he would feel more comfortable if I—"

"Not at all. I believe Rupert has heard something—some bit of gossip, perhaps, and if so, you are the very person to set the story straight."

Rupert turned red at these words and began to bluster. "Well, I must say . . . I mean, how . . . ? But you could not know. You are the most exasperating creature, Ursula. How could you possibly know that I have heard something?"

"Because I know you very well. You used to have that very expression on your face as a boy and had heard some bit of bad news about someone and were bursting to tell it. Now, do tell us what you have heard, and soon you will feel very much better."

He looked much beset and his eyes flew about the room as though seeking a way out of this uncomfortable situation. "Well, it was Albinia, actually," he muttered.

"Albinia," Ursula repeated encouragingly as he paused.

"Yes, you see, she had this letter from her friend Mrs. Cornwallis, who wrote of the most . . . the most outrageous stories concerning you, that I felt it my duty to come at once and . . . ah . . . learn the truth of these matters from your own lips."

"But I do not know a Mrs. Cornwallis. Why should she make up stories about me?" Ursula said in some confusion.

"More to the point," India said crisply, "is, where did Mrs. Cornwallis hear these outrageous stories?"

"Why, while she was staying with Lady Benbow recently."

"Ah!" Ursula and India exclaimed in unison.

"Yes. There was a relative of yours there, Lady Swanson, who had just come from a visit to you."

"My husband's cousin, Lord Herronly, Blanche Vernon."

"Just so."

"And what has Blanche been up to now?" Robert asked, strolling into the room.

"Oh, Robert, what a good thing you have come. This is Ursula's brother, Lord Herronly."

"How do you do, sir? Welcome to Swan Court."

"Thank you very much indeed, Lord Swanson. I hope you will forgive me for what I am about to reveal concerning your relative."

"Before you even begin, sir."

"Now, everyone sit down," India ordered. "Robert, Lord Herronly has come because he was greatly perturbed by some outrageous stories concerning Ursula that had been told him by his wife—at least, she did not learn the stories directly, but from a letter she had from a friend, Mrs. Cornwallis. Are you following all this?"

"Faintly pursuing," he said with a grin, for his wife's complicated way of explaining matters amused him very much.

"Yes, well, the letter came from this Mrs. Cornwallis, who had been staying with Lady Benbow, and the stories had been told to her by—"

"Blanche," her husband interrupted. "What did she say?"

"We were just getting to that part when you came in, dear. Lord Herronly is going to tell us now."

Three pairs of eyes turned expectantly upon poor Rupert, who became very flustered. "Well, I . . . It is very difficult for me to speak of such matters. I am very angry . . . I mean, how dare the woman . . . ? I beg your pardon, Lord Swanson, for speaking harshly of your cousin, but it is beyond my understanding how the woman could make such matters common gossip—"

"Blanche has never been known for her discretion," Robert said. "Please do not hesitate to say just what you like. We are all well-acquainted with Blanche's pretty ways here."

"Well, she said . . . oh, dear . . . she said that there was a young gentleman, a neighbor of yours, I think, who was pursued so relentlessly by Ursula that though he had only returned to his family after years in the West Indies, he was forced to flee to Bath to escape her attentions."

Ursula turned even paler than she had been, and India's eyes flashed a furious fire.

"Good God!" Robert exclaimed. "I would not have thought even Blanche could stoop to such a vicious lie as that."

"I shall never speak a civil word to her again as long as I live," India declared angrily.

"There is more," Rupert said unhappily.

"More!" The other three voices rose in unison.

"Yes, she also told Mrs. Cornwallis that a young man, also a guest in the house—"

"Lord Henry Somerton," Ursula said tightly.

"That . . . er . . . was his name, yes. Well, she said that he had also had to go away—for the same reason—and that . . . well, that you had pursued him to London, Ursula, and he had been forced to desert his sister there and leave to avoid you. Of course, I told Albinia this was all the grossest of lies, but I felt I must come myself to reassure her—that is, to reassure *you,* dear sister, that neither Albinia nor I believe one word of any of it, but . . ."

Suddenly Ursula and India, who had at first turned appalled eyes to one another, began to giggle. Once started, it was hard to stop, and they leaned back upon the sofa laughing helplessly, the tears rolling down their cheeks.

Rupert looked horrified. "It is hysterics? Should we do something?" he whispered to Robert.

"If there were a jug of water to hand, I would throw it over them," Robert said.

"Oh, dear," India said, sitting up and wiping her eyes. "Do forgive us, Lord Herronly. It is only that it is so . . . so completely and utterly ridiculous that one can only laugh. Oh, she is the most malicious, deceitful cat! I could cheerfully strangle her."

"Then it is all a farrago of lies, after all, just as I told Albinia."

"Well, not all lies," India said, causing Robert to look much alarmed. "She has the cast of characters right, it is just that she has rearranged the plot."

She then proceeded to tell him everything, leaving out only Ursula's feelings for Lord Henry and her own conviction that Lord Henry loved Ursula.

Rupert heard her out, only interjecting horrified exclamations from time to time. At last, when she had finished, he cried, "But this is beyond anything! If she were a man, I could call her out! It is slander of the worst sort, and I shall have to take her to court for so defaming the reputation of one of my family. Where is she to be found? I shall have my solicitors take action against her at once!"

"Oh, Rupert, I beg you will do no such thing!" Ursula cried. "Think of dragging all this through the courts—my name in the papers!"

"I agree," India said. "That would be too terrible for Ursula."

"Then I want to confront her myself with her lies and force her to write a retraction to Mrs. Cornwallis."

"Rupert, you would not last ten minutes with Blanche before she would have you convinced she was right after all." Then, seeing the affronted look on her brother's face, Ursula added, "If it were a man who had to be faced, you would have no trouble, but you know you are not good at standing up to women, especially if they begin to cry, which I am sure she would do. You know you are much too gallant to deny anything to a woman who cries.''

"If I may offer a suggestion, Lord Herronly," Robert interposed, "I believe I am the one person in this room who can stand up to Blanche with gloves on, ready to do battle. Blanche and I are old enemies, you see, and show each other no mercy. I ask that you allow me to handle this matter with her.''

"Well, I don't know, I'm sure . . . I think it is my duty. But on the other hand . . .''

"Exactly, sir. Would you by any chance have Mrs. Cornwallis' letter with you?''

"As a matter of fact''—Rupert reddened as he reached into an inner pocket—"it was so scandalous, I did not like having it lying about.''

"Ah, very good indeed. I think I shall quite enjoy myself. I should mention, sir, that Miss Vernon is at present a guest in this house," Robert said, causing Rupert's eyes to nearly pop out of his head as he looked around fearfully. "Not at my invitation, I may add. However, I can assure you she will no longer be, so you need not fear having to sit down to table with her. That being said, I hope we can persuade you to stay here for as long as you care to.''

"Too kind," Rupert murmured, much gratified. "Perhaps for a day or so. My wife suffers so from her nerves, you know, that I dare not be away too long.''

"We shall be very pleased to have you for as long as you can spare us. And now, if you will excuse me, I think it is best to settle this matter at once." Robert rose, bowed, and strode from the room, the light of battle in his eyes.

23

Robert knocked upon the front door of the Dower House and was admitted by his mother's new butler.

"Good day, m'lord. Lady Swanson and Miss Verson are in the drawing room."

He turned and led the way, threw open the door to announce Robert, then bowed him in and left, closing the door behind him. Robert sauntered across to his mother and bowed.

"Dearest boy, how delightful to see you. Do sit down."

"Thank you, Mama, but this is not a social call. I would like a few words with Blanche—alone," he said, turning at last to Blanche, but giving her no greeting.

"Of course, dearest, but surely you do not mean to turn me out of my own drawing room ? I am sure, whatever it is about, it is better for me to remain with Blanche in case—"

"Mama, I assure you we will not come to blows. If you will just step into the study for a few moments, Blanche."

"Oh, I had no use for a study, so I have turned it into my private sitting room now," the dowager said inconsequentially.

"It will serve my purposes under any name, Mama." He strode over to the door and opened it. "Blanche, if you please."

She stared at him for a few seconds and then shrugged and left the room.

They went wordlessly down the hall and into what had in

former days been the study. Blanche crossed to an upholstered chair and sat down, making a great to-do of arranging her skirts. When he still did not speak, she leaned back languidly and said, "Well?"

"We have a visitor at Swan Court. Lord Herronly, Ursula's brother."

"And you needed to give me this information privately?" she asked sarcastically.

"Not that, no. That is by way of setting the scene for what is to follow."

"How intriguing."

"I doubt you will find it so. Lord Herronly was very much disturbed by a letter his wife had received from a Mrs. Cornwallis."

Blanche, who had one hand to her head, fiddling with a curl, went absolutely still. After a long moment she lowered her arm carefully to her lap and said, "Mrs. Cornwallis. There are several ladies of that name."

"The Mrs. Cornwallis who was visiting Lady Benbow's while you were there," Robert said flatly.

"Oh, that one. Maria . . . Mrs. Holman Cornwallis. A very stupid woman."

"No doubt. But educated enough to write and repeat what she had been told. Since what she had been told concerned a relative of Lady Herronly's, Mrs. Cornwallis evidently thought she would be interested. I am sure by now you have realized what it is she had been told."

"Lord! There were ten other guests there. I was not a party to every conversation Mrs. Cornwallis had. I rather avoided the woman."

"Not enough, it seems. Better for you if you had."

"Please do not speak to me in those threatening tones, Robert. I will not stand for it."

"Then you had best remain seated. Mrs. Cornwallis named you in her letter as the source of the stories she wrote to Lady Herronly."

"Then she lies. I barely spoke to the woman."

"You spoke enough to tell a whole tarradiddle about Ursula Liddiard, however. For instance, that she pursued Sir Tarquin so relentlessly that he was forced to flee to Bath."

"He did go to Bath!"

"Only after he had proposed to Ursula and been refused."

"He proposed to that plain little creature? And she refused him? I do not believe it."

"Nevertheless, it is the truth. What is not the truth is that she pursued him, and you knew that very well. You followed up that lie with a second—that she was also trying to attach Lord Henry's interest and that he left to escape her attentions, after which she followed him to London."

"She did! She did! My aunt said so!" Blanche cried shrilly.

"But you knew Lord Henry was not in London and that Ursula only went at his sister's pressing invitation. I am sure my mother told you that, as well as insinuated her own interpretation of the facts."

"She has a right to her own opinion."

"So she always says to explain her blunders. Nevertheless, you were there at the time and you had plenty of opportunity to observe, and you are not stupid, whatever else you are. You know that Ursula Liddiard never pursued anyone as you described to Mrs. Cornwallis."

"Much good it would do her if she did," Blanche said nastily.

"That is your opinion. She did, however, receive an offer from Sir Tarquin, which is more than you managed to accomplish despite your relentless and blatant efforts to attach him."

"And Lord Henry?" Blanche sneered.

"It is my opinion Ursula will be Lady Henry Somerton before the year is out," Robert replied calmly, armed with his belief in his wife's intuition in the matter.

Blanche's mouth thinned to a grim line. "You will pardon me if I take leave to doubt that."

"Certainly, doubt away if it makes you feel better. But we are straying from the point. That being that you told these deliberate lies to the woman, not caring a whit what damage they might do an innocent girl's reputation, or who might be hurt."

"I deny it absolutely."

"I have Mrs. Cornwallis' letter to Lady Herronly in my pocket, Blanche." She lost some color at this, but remained mulishly silent. "In that letter she names you as the person who told her, and says that you should know of what you speak, since you were staying at Swan Court at the time and observed it all. Surely she would have no reason to lie about that. Apart from that, we both know there was no one else at Lady Benbow's who was also a guest at Swan Court. It is no good, Blanche."

She stared at him balefully for a time, then rose and said, "I have a headache. I am weary of this very timesome conversation."

"So am I. In fact, the whole business makes me feel nauseated. But I am not finished. You will write to Mrs. Cornwallis today—at once—and tell her you were misinformed and there was not a word of truth in anything you said. I will read the letter and take it with me to post when I leave."

"I will do no such thing."

"If you do not, I will feel it my duty to write to her and to Lady Benbow, telling them of your true character. As well as any other of my friends who I feel might be injured by being exposed to your vicious tongue."

"You would not!" Blanche cried, horrified.

"Try me. You are a blight, Blanche, spreading unhappiness around you wherever you go. I will not allow you to go on unchecked. No bad deed goes unpunished, you will find, and I intend this one to be punished if I am forced to do it myself."

"Oh, please do not be so self-righteous. You make me sick!"

"The feeling is entirely mutual. Now, will you write the letter or shall I?"

"All right, all right, all right! I see there is no way to be rid of you until I do." She rose and strode angrily across the room to her aunt's escritoire, where she pulled out paper and pen and began to write rapidly:

Dear Mrs. Cornwallis,
    I have learned that those things I told you at Lady Benbow's were untrue. I was misinformed, I fear. I hope you will not repeat any of it until I have the opportunity to learn the truth. I will write again soon and tell you.
    In haste, your friend,

                                    Blanche Vernon

"There," she said, nearly throwing the paper at Robert. "I hope you are satisfied."

He read it through slowly. "It will do." He handed it back with the request that she fold it and put Mrs. Cornwallis' direction on it. "Do not seal it. I want to show the letter to Ursula and her brother before it is posted."

"I shall never speak to you again!" she declared, her teeth grating with frustration and fury.

"I shall do everything in my power to assist you in keeping your word," he replied coolly.

"And I shall never step one foot inside your gates again."

"Ah, yes, I was just coming to that. Since Lord Herronly is staying with us, and Ursula now knows of your perfidy, it will not be possible for you to return there."

She said through clenched teeth, "Have my abigail pack and bring my things to me here. I hope you will allow one of your carriages to bring her."

"Nothing will give me greater pleasure," he said sardonically, then turned and left the room without another word.

The dowager came hurrying into the hall when she heard her son's footsteps. "Oh, Robert, what is going on? You have been so long. Please do not treat your mother in this way. You know I cannot bear mysteries."

"I am sure Blanche will tell you, but do not believe anything she says, the truth is foreign to her nature."

"My son, how can you speak of dear Blanche so?" she said reproachfully.

"Because I know her ways. I have just caught her in a tissue of lies concerning Ursula, which she has been forced to retract. I will say no more, since you are fond of her. And for that very reason she will now become your guest instead of mine, for I cannot any longer entertain her in my home."

"But this is dreadful!"

"I fear I cannot look upon it in that light. However, you have a fully furnished room for her, as well as staff. She will have to stay here."

"Then I shall have to stay with her. I could not possibly allow her to remain here alone."

"That is as you wish, Mama. You were going to remove here in any case in a few days, were you not?"

"But my dinner! Nothing has been ordered!"

"Oh, for heaven's sake, Mama, surely your cook can put together a simple meal for you. There will be only the two of you. You will not need three full courses!" Robert replied with some irritation.

By the time he had entered his own drawing room again, however, his irritation had been soothed away, to be replaced by a feeling of great satisfaction in having finally said all the things he had wanted to say to Blanche and bent her to his will, in a manner of speaking, so he could rest assured that he would never have to entertain her in his own home again.

Three pairs of anxious eyes turned toward him. "Well,

we may all be easy," he said lightly. "I have a letter in my pocket from Blanche to Mrs. Cornwallis, admitting that her stories were all lies. I also have Blanche's assurance that she will never speak to me or step foot inside my gates again. One could not ask for more."

"Oh, Robert, you are wonderful," India cried, flinging herself into his arms. "Was she very difficult?"

"Blanche does not give way all at once, but today she was eventually forced to do as I asked her, having no recourse," he replied just a shade boastfully.

Lord Herronly wrung Robert's hand with great enthusiasm, and Ursula put her arms about his neck and kissed his cheek. "I really can never thank you enough for standing up for me, Robert."

"You are my friend, so I had no trouble at all," he said simply. The tears rose in her eyes and she kissed his cheek again. "Now, then, to business. India, will you see that Blanche's maid packs all her things as soon as possible, and I will order a carriage to take her to the Dower House. And I suppose you had better send Mama's maid with her night things at the same time, for she says she cannot leave Blanche there alone. Come, Lord Herronly, we will descend to the cellars."

"The cellars, Robert? Whatever can you want down there?"

"Well, I think the occasion calls for something very special in the way of wine. When we have all finished our tasks, I shall ask you all to drink my health, for I have faced the dragon and slain it."

24

The party left at Swan Court seemed, to all outward appearances, content. Robert was satisfied with himself for having at last established his mother somewhere other than in his own home and for having, hopefully, rid himself of Blanche. Her letter to Mrs. Cornwallis had been safely dispatched the same day it was written, and he hoped Blanche's credit would suffer with some of her friends, at least.

India was happy to see her husband contented, and, secure in her belief in Lord Henry's love for Ursula, relieved to think that soon her friend would hear him tell her of it himself.

Rupert was euphoric to have what could have been a dreadful scandal, causing much misery for his sister and her family, completely discounted, his sister's good name vindicated, and the perpetrator of the scandal punished. He had written at once to Albinia with all this good news, and several days later she had replied that Mrs. Cornwallis had just written to her, and had enclosed Blanche's note of retraction, as well as the good news that Mrs. Cornwallis had been in bed for nearly two weeks with a very bad cold and had seen no one, which meant that she had not been able to spread Blanche's stories among her acquaintance. Albinia ended by reminding him that he had already been gone from home five days and that his children were very upset not to have their papa with them.

Remembering this as he rode along beside Ursula gave

him a pang of guilt, but he quickly pushed it aside and
engaged in conversation with his sister. He rarely had
occasion to escape the entanglement of wife and children that
bound him close to home, and he was enjoying himself
immensely. Youngreaves had a really first-rate cellar, his
lady had an excellent cook, and Rupert was freed of the
fretful calls of his nervous wife and the badgering of his
unruly brood of children. He decided he would stay at least
two more days, with the excuse that he was not entirely
satisfied with his sister's state of health. She looked pale and
unhappy, and though she spoke cheerfully enough, it seemed
to him it was with some effort. He had questioned India about
this, but she had only murmured that Ursula was perhaps
still weary from her long years of nursing.

"But she had nothing really to tire her, there were plenty
of servants to help her," Rupert expostulated.

"There can grow upon a young girl a great weariness of
spirit from having to sit for hours with a person of unhappy
temperament, ailing to death. And it was not just for a few
months, but five long, empty years with no friends about
her, no amusements, none of the things a young girl in her
position has every right to expect."

He was quelled and said no more, but his love for his sister
had grown much deeper from that point. He hovered about
her, holding chairs, finding pillows for her back, handing
her her cup of tea solicitously, even insisting upon taking
her candle and accompanying her to her room each evening,
to plant a loving kiss upon her brow at her door.

He stole a glance at her now as he jogged along happily
on the mount Robert had found for him. She had a touch
of color in her cheeks as usual when she rode, but the smile
she turned upon him did not touch her eyes, and it seemed
a sad smile to him.

"My dear," he said impulsively, "I hope you feel that
you can confide in me if there is anything wrong?"

"Of course I do, Rupert. How good you are to me. But
I assure you I have nothing to confide. I am happy to see

you going along so well with Robert," she added to change the direction of his thoughts.

"Ah, an excellent fellow, excellent! I wish we were neighbors so that I might see more of him."

He went on at length about the fine qualities of his host, while Ursula listened attentively and responded to keep her mind from exploring her unhappiness any further. It had now been five days since she had received Elizabeth's letter, and no further word had been heard concerning Lord Henry's movements. Ursula could not rid herself of her belief that Miss Devere still held him enchanted at the Alvanleys', despite what he had written to his sister.

Feeling this, she could not believe that with her lifelong habit of practical good sense, she could not order her mind and set about getting on with her life. She told herself again and again that she had no intention of going into a decline like some heroine of a romantic novel over an unreturned love. After all, it was only a first love, and everyone knew they were usually only infatuations soon over. This was only an extension of that mild infatuation she had felt for Lord Henry during her first Season. It had been forcibly put into storage all these years and now had come feebly to life again only because these girlish feelings had been roused by the romantic way he had been, quite literally, thrown across her path.

All of these things were very clear in her mind, and when she sternly rehearsed them to herself, her chin always came up and her spine straightened in physical exhibition of her firm resolves. In between times, or when she was off her guard, a small voice reminded her drearily, "It is now three days," "It is now four days," "It is now five days."

Henry was saying almost the same words to himself, only in great exasperation. He had set forth with wildly beating heart and great hopes from the Alvanleys' on the two-day journey to Poynton's that had, through a visitation of mishaps, already extended itself into four days. First a wheel had inexplicably broken on the first day, which entailed a four-mile walk to the next village to find men to send back to repair it. This took so much of the day that the carriage arrived at the inn where he waited only as dusk was falling, so departure had to be put off until the next day. Though he made an early start then, there had been heavy rain just before dawn, and besides the plague of mired roads which slowed progress sometimes to a standstill, about midday two hours were wasted removing a very large tree that had been struck by lightning and fallen across the road. The third day, better progess was made, but he still arrived at Poynton's door only in the late afternoon of the fourth day.

There, to his dismay, he found his friend in a very sad state, for he had been thrown from his horse two days before and broken his collarbone. His mood, never one of great amiability, was now verging on the curmudgeonly. Henry felt it would be too unkind to rush away on the very first day of his visit, so he resigned himself to a fifth day of delay.

The dowager had appeared at Swan Court on the day after Robert's encounter with Blanche, in great agitation and demanding that her son accompany her into the library for an interview.

"Robert, I insist upon knowing what happened yesterday. Blanche will only say it was a great bit of nonsense and she does not wish to discuss it. I *will* know what this is all about. You know I cannot bear any discord. I feel sure I can put things right between you if I am only apprised of the facts."

"I fear that will never be possible, Mama, but you shall hear the facts if you insist." He thereupon told her the sordid tale of Blanche's misdoings.

The dowager looked appalled at first, but then she rallied. "I cannot believe dear Blanche would tell such deliberate falsehoods," she declared stoutly.

"Mama, she has told lies since I can first remember. A great many about me, which somehow you always managed to make yourself believe, even though I was your son and had never told you a falsehood."

"But I . . . I cannot bring myself to believe—"

"Again you disbelieve me," he reminded her gently. "Where does this faith in Blanche come from? She has never been particularly good to you that I have seen, and at times she treats you quite unkindly."

"That . . . that is just her way, and I pay it no mind, but surely you . . . surely she would not . . . you must be mistaken, dear boy, I cannot believe she would do such a thing. She . . . she . . ." She halted in frustration, torn between her two loyalties.

"She wrote the retraction, Mama. She would not have done that had she been innocent."

"But she would not dream that woman would repeat—"

"That does not change the fact that what she told the woman were all lies, and you know very well that anyone who will listen to gossip will repeat it. However, I have told you everything and you must do as you like about it. You will excuse me now, Mama, I have a meeting with my factor."

He left the room quickly before she could protest, and she sat there for some time puzzling her mind to find some extenuating circumstance to excuse Blanche's behavior. Poor woman, she was sorely tried, for she was so accustomed to thinking of Blanche as all she would have wanted in a daughter of her own that she had become quite blind to her faults.

Presently she went upstairs to oversee the packing of her things for removal to the Dower House and managed to put the whole disagreeable episode from her mind, for she was not given to introspection.

Unfortunately, her ideas of what were her things and what belonged to the house were dim. She came each day, and India was at last apprised by her housekeeper that an unusual number of things had been reported missing by the maids whose duty it was to dust and clean each morning.

" . . . and 'tis not the maids taking them, that I will swear to. Fine girls from honest homes, they are, and would never have told me of it had they been taking things themselves.

Besides, I had a look through their rooms just to be sure. 'Twas only noticed in the last few days, m'lady,'' the house-keeper said significantly, emphasizing her last few words, for she had her own ideas about where the things were going.

India knew as well, for she had seen her mother-in-law going quickly upstairs just the day before with a small silver epergne from the dining room. She had started to call out to her, much puzzled as to why she was taking it upstairs, but then realized the truth. She had shrugged it off, however, determined that she would not interfere in any way or speak to Robert about it. She was not willing to be the agent for more trouble between her husband and his mother.

Robert, however, learned of his mother's small thefts for himself when he entered the hall unexpectedly one day and heard his mother's voice raised angrily from the small drawing room. He went to the door and opened it quietly.

'' . . . what do you mean you will speak to his lordship?'' the dowager was saying to Crigly. ''How dare you speak so to me? I want that clock put in my carriage at once or *I* will speak to his lordship!''

''Speak to me about what, Mama?'' Robert asked.

The dowager started violently and whipped around toward him, her mouth hanging open in shock. A wash of red rose up her throat to her hairline, and guilt replaced the look of shock.

''I . . . I . . . Goodness, my son, how you startled me! I wish you would not creep about the house in such a way,'' she cried defensively.

''That will be all, Crigly,'' Robert said. The butler bowed and left the room, closing the door firmly behind himself. ''Now, what is this all about, Mama? I believe I heard you asking Crigly to carry this clock to your carriage, did I not?''

''No, I . . . I mean . . . well, yes, you did—it is one of my most cherished wedding gifts.''

''Why, Mama, you know Papa's grandfather brought the clock back from France when he returned from his honey-moon,'' he said chidingly.

"You are mistaken, Robert. My Aunt Lavinia gave me the clock at my wedding," the dowager maintained stubbornly.

The clock in question was of French enamel, pale green in color and lavishly decorated with shepherds, shepherdesses, and cherubs. It had stood on the mantel in this room for well over a hundred years, as they both knew.

"I dislike this squabbling, Mama. Please let us drop the subject. If you want the clock, I will give it to you."

"It belongs to me, I tell you!"

"Then you shall have it. I do wonder, however, why Papa should have told me otherwise." He crossed to the door. "Crigly," he called, "please carry this clock to Lady Swanson's carriage. Good afternoon, Mama." He bowed politely and left.

Crigly entered the room, bowed gravely to the dowager, and crossing to the fireplace, reached up to the clock.

"Never mind, I have changed my mind. I do not think it will suit the Dower House, after all." Chin in the air, the dowager turned and stalked out of the room. Crigly allowed himself just the smallest of smiles.

25

There were no further depredations upon the furnishings at Swan Court. The French clock ticked away serenely upon the mantelpiece in the small drawing room. However, a priceless yellow Chinese vase of unimaginable antiquity, two valuable gem-set snuffboxes, the silver epergne, two paintings—one a Thomas Lawrence of Robert's aunt as a girl, the other a vista by Turner—a chased-silver punch bowl, and the twenty matching cups had all found a new home at the Dower House.

No references were made to any of these things to the dowager, who continued to call when she felt inclined to do so, and usually these visits were to ask for things: a basket of peaches or grapes from the hothouses; some veal cutlets for Blanche's dinner, since the dear girl craved them and it was too late to get them from the butcher; great bouquets of flowers, cut for her unwillingly by a grumbling gardener; fresh peas from the kitchen garden, since her own gardens had been so sadly let go while the Dower House was untenanted.

Blanche, of course, never accompanied her aunt on these calls. She trailed around the Dower House at an extremity of boredom, and having had no responses to several letters to friends proposing herself for a visit, had no place to escape to except to her own home, where she would be even more bored. At least here there was Mr. Phillips-Glenn-Phillips, while at home there was no one for miles except her parents' elderly friends, all married. She thought that pride would make it impossible to accept a proposal of marriage from Mr. Phillips-Glenn-Phillips, for she could not bear to become a laughingstock, but she would like very much to prove to herself that her charms were still potent by receiving his proposal. She wished that he would come now while her aunt was at Swan Court. Perhaps if they were alone together he would screw up his courage at last.

However, he did not come that day at all, but arrived quite early the following morning, and flustered the dowager by requesting a private interview with her. Why, the old-fashioned darling, Blanche thought gleefully, he is going to ask her permission to address me. She hugged herself and danced about the breakfast table. Perhaps I will have him after all, she thought, he is so very rich! Why, I could have my own carriage, a whole stable of riding horses, all the gowns I want, jewels!

While she was enumerating these desirable things to herself, Mr. Phillips-Glenn-Phillips was asking the dowager in a very high-flown, courtly manner for the honor of her hand in marriage.

"I . . . I beg your pardon, sir. Surely . . . you mean Blanche . . ."

He laughed gently. "No, madam. I hope I would never do anything so unseemly as to court a girl young enough to be my daughter. I have tried to be kind to her for your sake, but what I seek in marriage is peace and companionship for my remaining years, and it is my belief we could offer each other those things."

"Well, sir, you quite take my breath away. I cannot hide my amazement from you. I never dreamed of such a thing."

"I hope now, however, you will consider it. I believe we would suit very well."

There was a long moment of silence while the dowager considered. "Mr. Phillips, I cannot accept your offer," she said at last. "I am, naturally, very flattered by it, but I have no wish to marry again."

"Dear lady, could you not give the matter more thought?"

"No, I am sorry, but I have no need for more thought. I like my life just as it is, now I have settled in so well here. Marriage would change everything, and I have no wish for that sort of change."

Mr. Phillips-Glenn-Phillips had nothing to do but accept her decision gracefully and depart. The dowager had the bad judgment to report the interview to Blanche, who at once turned perfectly white and then went into a blind fury. They were in the breakfast room, where the dowager had returned to find her niece, and at her news Blanche picked up a cut-crystal bowl of fruit from the table and flung it at the tiled fireplace, where it shattered into a million sparkling bits.

The dowager was so stunned by this violence that she was struck dumb and could only gape at the shattered bowl, while Blanche began to rant. It took some time for the dowager to take in what her niece was saying as she recovered her senses slowly.

" . . . marry you! You! That is obscene! You are too old and certainly have no looks left. Why? Why? Why? What could he want with you? He has all the money he needs. No, no, it was me he wanted, and you in your usual stupid way have muddled everything. I know he could not want you . . . " The dowager turned white at such savage, unkind words.

After a few moments of it, however, the color began returning as she became angry and her eyes began to take on a fierce glitter. When Blanche at last collapsed upon a chair, sobbing and laughing hysterically at the same time, the dowager calmly picked up a jug of water and dashed it into the girl's face.

The noise stopped abruptly and Blanche stared at her aunt in disbelief, the water streaming from her face and hair. "How dare you," she gasped.

"I dare a great many things. For instance, I dare to dislike being spoken of to my face in such a disrespectful way. I dare resent having my property flung about and destroyed.

And I daresay it is time you returned to your parents for a course in good manners.''

Blanche rose, and drawing the tattered rags of her dignity about her, said grandly, "I had already come to the decision to leave here. I cannot bear another hour of this tedious boredom." She stalked from the room and, indeed, departed the next day, after demanding the loan of her aunt's carriage to convey her to her parents. The dowager had to consent to this because she knew her sister would never forgive her if Blanche were forced to travel in a public conveyance.

Henry, meanwhile, had spent an obligatory day consoling and entertaining his old friend, and at the end of it explained that on the morrow he was obliged to pay a call upon the Youngreaves and would most probably be away all day. He apologized for his desertion, to which Poynton only grunted. At breakfast the next morning, however, he was uncharacteristically loquacious, making it impossible, without downright rudeness, for Henry to get away before ten. As he was going only seven miles, he was not unduly perturbed by this, and at last set off on horseback for Swan Court.

He did not push his horse, for though impatient, he was also somewhat anxious about his reception. Perhaps since he had last seen her, Ursula had met some other gentleman and given her heart to him, or not met anyone, but still felt no particular regard for himself. He had thought she had some regard for young Rochdale, having seen her blushing self-consciousness in his presence, and yet it seemed he was wrong and she had refused the man's offer of marriage. Elizabeth had said she had seemed unhappy in London, but that might have been owing to regret at refusing Rochdale, or any number of other reasons, none of them having to do with himself and his abrupt departure from Swan Court, as Elizabeth had hinted.

By the time he reached his destination, he had completely blue-deviled himself and was on the point of turning back, and might have done so had he not been overtaken by Robert, who hailed him with great warmth.

As they entered the hall, Robert called out, "India, you can never guess who has come to visit!" as he led Henry to the drawing room.

"Oh, is it Lord Henry?" she called back, hope and disbelief mingling in her voice.

"You minx! How did you guess?" Robert said as he entered the room and crossed to kiss his wife's auburn curls, haloed to flame by a ray of sun.

India did not rise, for getting out of chairs made her look awkward, she thought, but she beamed up at him and held out her hands to Henry.

"Dear Lord Henry, how well you are looking! We are so pleased that you have come to see us. Your sister wrote that you were coming into the neighborhood, and we did hope you would not forget us."

"As though I ever could, after all your great kindness to me. You and Robert are both looking flourishing, I am happy to say." He looked about the room. "Where . . . ah . . . ?"

"Well, Robert's mama has moved to the Dower House, and Blanche, who went to Lady Benbow's for a visit just after you left, had returned and was staying there for a time, but has now returned home." She paused and gave him a mischievous glance. "Oh, and Ursula is out riding. Ah, but here is someone you will like to meet," she said as Rupert entered the room. "Lord Herronly, Ursula's brother. Lord Henry Somerton, Rupert."

The gentlemen shook hands, looking upon each other with curiosity, Rupert because this was the man his sister had picked up unconscious from the road, Henry because this was Ursula's relative.

"Lord Herronly usually rides with Ursula, but today she said she would like to be alone. I expect she will return shortly, do you not, Lord Herronly?"

"Lord, yes. She has been out nearly two hours already."

"Well, Ursula usually likes long rides," India replied complacently. She felt like a fat cat who has just consumed an entire pint of cream, and could barely conceal the smugness of her smile. With Lord Henry here at last, she could no longer doubt her earlier convictions. She had been right all along, and wanted very much to whisper to Robert, "I told you so." True, these past two days had caused some flagging of those convictions, but she ignored that now.

A light luncheon had been ordered, and though Ursula had not returned, Robert suggested that he felt somewhat sharp set, so they went in to be served. Lord Henry only toyed with his food, claiming he rarely ate in the middle of the day. He told them of the missed letters from his sister, owing to his changes of plan, and how sorry he had been not to have seen Lady Ursula in London. He spoke of the irritating delays of his journey upon leaving the Alvanleys', and of the sad state of health in which he had found his friend Poynton, necessitating another day's delay in coming to pay his respects to the Youngreaves once he was in the neighborhood, which had, of course, been his first object.

India looked around, as though to exchange a telling but unrevealing look with her absent friend, and met Robert's eye. He raised one eyebrow infinitesimally, which she was happy to find did just as well. She responded in kind and turned her attention back to her guests.

Rupert had instituted inquiries of friends from Henry's part of the country, and Henry responded politely, but it was clear his heart was not in it. Each time the door opened to admit a servant, he looked up expectantly and then away, barely concealing his disappointment. What could be keeping the girl? Why was no one worried by her long absence?

When they rose from the table, Robert said he had estate business and excused himself. Henry at once said he felt the need for exercise and would go for a ride, a patent fiction for someone who had already ridden seven miles that day. Rupert opened his mouth, but India at once laid a hand on his arm and begged him so prettily to accompany her to the hothouse to give her some advice about her peaches that he agreed at once. She knew he had been on the point of saying he would go with Lord Henry, but she guessed that Lord

Henry was going in search of Ursula, and would do much better, if he found her, if her brother was not present to witness the meeting.

"You might come upon Ursula in that copse just over the rise when you turn left out of the stables. She often stops there before she comes home," she said over her shoulder as she led Rupert away.

Ursula had indeed stopped in the copse after her long ride. Seeing a small glade ahead that she had not yet explored, she swung herself to the ground, looped the reins over a low bush, and wandered slowly forward. The grass was thick and inviting, and a small rise offered comfort for her back, so she sat for a time, pulling at grass spears and winding them about her fingers. She had traveled that morning through the final stages of despair and reached the quieter shore of resignation. It was now a week, and she knew that all the hopes raised by Elizabeth's letter—despite her disbelief in any hope—were now proved false and were dead. Anger and grief were now behind her, and she felt only a great weariness. At last she lay back against the small rise and stared up at the deep blue showing through the trees, the breeze dappling sun and leaf shadow over her eyes until at last they closed and without even realizing it she fell deeply asleep.

Henry rode left out of the stables as directed, over the rise, and at last into the copse. He looked about eagerly as he rode, hoping to espy Ursula among the trees, but saw no sign of her. It was very quiet among the trees, and cool, with only the softest of breezes blowing.

After a time he came upon the glade and saw her at last, flat on her back, one arm raised above her head, the other flung out to the side. He felt his heart leap into his throat with shock and horror. She had been thrown! She was dead! Then he became aware of the sound of tearing grass, and a quick glance showed him her mare cropping grass some distance away. In an instant he flung himself to the ground and ran to kneel beside the still, beloved form. He gathered her into his arms, murmuring brokenly, "Oh, darling girl . . . dearest Ursula . . . please . . . don't be dead."

He suddenly thought to feel for signs of life, and put his hand to the side of her throat. Just as he realized he was feeling a steady and very healthy pulse there, her eyes opened slowly and stared up bewilderedly into the face bent so near her own.

"Henry? Oh, yes, I see. I am dreaming," she said as though to herself.

Her sleep-filled blue eyes, nearly violet in this shaded place, filled him with such joy that he snatched her as closely into his arms as possible. "No, my darling, not a dream. Do you mind?"

"Why . . . no, I do not mind, but . . . but . . ." She was still in a sleepy daze, and her usual calm was not yet in place.

"Do you . . . can you love me, Ursula?" he whispered, his face buried in her hair.

"Why, yes, of course, but . . ."

He groaned and brought his face to hers and kissed her bruisingly and at length. When at last he released her, she said breathlessly, "But . . . but do you . . . ?"

"Need you ask?" he cried wonderingly.

"Yes," she said simply."

"Oh, you stupid, darling girl," he said with a shaky laugh. He then proceeded to tell her what she needed to know, demonstrating his words with increasing frequency as he went along, until at last the words were lost and only the demonstration continued.